ROBERT ROWS
THE RIVER

WEEKLY READER CHILDREN'S BOOK CLUB · INTERMEDIATE DIVISION

By the Same Author

Published by William Morrow and Company

Published by Harcourt, Brace and World

Weekly Reader Children's Book Club

Presents

ROBERT ROWS THE RIVER

written and illustrated by
CAROLYN HAYWOOD

William Morrow and Company
New York

To

the Radcliffes of "Woodlawn," Staines,
and especially to Alan.

CONTENTS

ROBERT ROWS
THE RIVER

Chapter One

ACROSS THE RIVER

THE back of the house where Robert lived with his father and mother looked onto the River Thames. This meant that the largest river in England was in Robert's backyard. As other children watching from their windows saw cars and buses pass, so Robert watched all kinds of boats going up and down the river.

Robert had ridden in boats as long as he could remember. Ever since he had started to school he had ridden in the family rowboat every morning, for his mother had to row him across the river. On the other side he waited for Mrs. Wiggins, who drove him the rest of the way to his school. Robert was the last one of five boys that Mrs. Wiggins picked up.

The winter that Robert was eight years old the river had frozen over and, for several weeks, he had walked across the river to meet Mrs. Wiggins.

Now Robert was nine and it was holiday time. For five long weeks there would be no morning hurry to get across the river before Mrs. Wiggins arrived. Instead, Robert could spend as much time as he wished in the rowboat. He could handle the oars as well as his mother, and he liked nothing better than exploring the banks of the Thames, keeping a sharp lookout for little treasures that had been washed in from the river. His father called it "river ratting," but Robert said his treasures were "all sorts of useful things." After a while his father and mother began to call them Robert's "all sorts."

Once he had found a wooden wheel floating in the river. He rowed around the rest of the morning, hoping he would find another. Just as he was about to give up the search another wheel floated by, and Robert was able to pull it in. These "all sorts" were exactly what he needed to make a little wagon. When Robert had the wagon finished it made a very strange noise on the brick walk, because the wheels were not quite even. It went, *Kronk! Kronk! Kronk!* So ever after the wagon was called Kronk.

Sometimes Robert took his friends Timothy and Jeffrey with him in the rowboat. They were twins who lived on the opposite side of the river. But Timothy and Jeffrey never seemed to find anything very exciting. It was only when Robert went alone that he found things that were worth keeping.

This morning Robert sat in the rowboat under the great weeping-willow tree that grew on the bank of the river. It was one of three willow trees that were so large they almost filled the entire garden.

They towered above Robert's house, carrying their branches high into the air and dropping them like a green waterfall almost to the ground.

Robert loved to sit in the boat surrounded by the curtain of green leaves. It was one of his special hideouts. Here the rowboat was rocked gently by the water, dark green where it reflected the willow tree and splashed with gold where the sun shone through the leaves. He listened to the *lap, lap* of the river against the boat and the nearby shore.

He looked up into the branches of the big tree. There was the tree house his father had built for him. Now that Robert was free from school he would spend a lot of time in the tree house. In fact, his friends from across the river were coming this morning for a picnic in it.

Daisy, who lived on the other side of the river near the twins, was bringing currant buns for everyone. Daisy's mother made the best currant buns Robert had ever eaten. He hoped there would be plenty of butter on them. Robert's mouth began to water as he thought of the buns. He looked at his wristwatch. It was still too early to go for his friends.

When they arrived they would put the currant buns into the tree-house basket, together with the milk that Robert's mother always provided. Then they would all climb the ladder up to the tree house and haul up the basket.

Hauling the basket up to the tree house was always exciting. Everyone shouted directions. "Do it slowly! Not so fast! Don't tip it! You're tipping it! Careful! You're going to knock it against that branch!" But the basket always came up, and so far nothing had been spilled out.

Robert looked over the side of the boat down into the water. He looked along the bank to see if anything interesting had washed up. Occasionally he peeked out between the slits in the leafy curtain. It was fun to see and not be seen. A large pleasure boat passed, and Robert heard the voices of the people crowding the deck. After it had gone its wake rocked the rowboat and splashed a little water over the side. A tiny drop, struck by the sunlight, looked like a diamond as it flew toward Robert. He reached out and caught it in his hand. He held it tight and sat for a moment making believe he had a real diamond.

He soon forgot about the diamond, for a houseboat came in sight. A boy and a girl were standing on the deck sucking lollipops. The sun had tanned the children a rich golden brown. It had bleached their blond heads a pale straw color. Robert thought it would be wonderful to live on a houseboat and travel up and down the river. The children were living like the Gypsies, who traveled around in brightly painted wagons. The houseboat passed out of sight before Robert could decide which would be more fun, a houseboat or a Gypsy wagon.

Now as Robert looked out through his green lace curtain he saw some of the river's swans. He counted five of the snow-white birds. They were coming

toward him like a flotilla of small white ships. Robert sat very still. He knew why they were coming. They were coming to the willow tree, for the water under it held little bugs that the swans relished. Robert watched them as they swam outside his curtain, dipping their long curving necks into the water.

When the swans glided away Robert looked at his watch. It was getting close to eleven o'clock, almost time to row across to pick up his friends. It was such a short way straight across the river, and such a long way if one walked to the bridge and back along the road, that he always rowed over to get them. Robert watched for the children. Although he would be able to see them, they could not see him, for he was hidden by the leafy curtain of the willow tree. When he was sure they were looking for him, he would part the curtain and row out.

Robert kept his eyes on the far bank. In a few minutes he saw Jeffrey running from his house. In a moment Timothy appeared. Then a shout from

Jeffrey carried across the river. "Hello, Daisy!"

Robert watched Daisy as she opened a paper bag that she was carrying. Jeffrey looked inside. "There are the currant buns," said Robert to himself. He saw Timothy look into the bag, and then suddenly the three children turned away from the river. Someone had called to them.

Robert pushed his boat out from under the willow tree and waved to his friends. They were now running up and down the towpath, waving their arms and hands. They jumped up and down and shouted, but a breeze carried the sound away. Robert waved his arms in the air and shouted, "I'm coming!" He swung the boat about and, with his back to the opposite shore, began to row. Robert rowed hard. Dip-pull! Dip-pull! At last he reached the little dock on the other side of the river. He wondered why his friends were so very quiet. Usually they were shouting, "Hello, Robby! Hello!"

Robert looked around. No one was there. He

looked up on the bank where they usually waited for him, but he saw nothing but a brown paper bag. Picnickers! Always leaving paper bags around, Robert thought to himself. He called out, "Jeff! Tim!" There was no answer. He tried calling Daisy. There was no reply.

That's very funny, thought Robert. Then in a moment he said aloud. "No, it's not very funny. I've come all the way over for them and now they're hiding." He put his hands to his mouth and shouted, "Hello!"

A faint cry came back, "Hello!" To Robert's great surprise, it came from across the river. He looked back at his own shore and there were his three friends, running back and forth, waving their arms around, and behaving just the way they had when he had been over there and they had been over here. They were all shouting at once, but he could not understand what they were saying.

Robert turned the boat around and began to row

back. When he reached his dock the three children were waiting for him. "How did you get over?" said Robert. "And why didn't you wait for me?"

"We got a lift!" shouted Jeffrey. "The bread man was coming over the bridge and he brought us along."

"We told you not to come," said Timothy.

"I couldn't hear you," said Robert.

"And you didn't bring the bag of currant buns," said Daisy. "Didn't you hear us calling to you to bring the currant buns?"

"Where are they?" said Robert, looking puzzled.

"I put them down to tie my shoelace and I forgot them," Daisy replied.

"That's what we were trying to tell you," said Timothy.

"I couldn't hear you," said Robert. "Now I'll have to go back for the currant buns."

"We'll come with you," the children said in a chorus.

When they had climbed into the boat, Robert turned the boat around once more. He started back across the river. Dip-pull! Dip-pull!

About halfway across Daisy suddenly cried out, "Oh! There's Blackie!"

The children all knew who Blackie was. He was a big black dog who lived up the road. "Oh! He's snooping around!" Daisy cried. "Oh! He'll find the bag of currant buns!" Daisy was so excited she almost stood up in the boat.

"Sit still, Daisy!" Robert called out. "Don't get up. You might upset the boat."

"Try and pull harder, Robby!" said Timothy, who was watching Blackie as he got closer to the bag of currant buns.

"I can't," said Robert.

"Hurry! Hurry!" Daisy called out. "He's almost to the bag."

Timothy and Jeffrey began to shout at the dog. "Go home! Go home!"

Blackie paid no attention. He just nosed closer to the bag of currant buns.

Finally Robert brought the boat to the dock. Timothy jumped out and ran to the bag of buns just as Blackie reached them. "Get off!" said Timothy, as he picked up the bag. Blackie ran away and Timothy rushed back to the boat.

"Give them here," said Robert, "so you don't drop them in the river." Timothy handed the bag to Robert. Robert looked in the bag, and said, "Oh, don't they look good."

"We can't eat them here," said Daisy. "They're to eat in the tree house."

Robert handed the bag to Daisy. "Well, all right," he sighed, "but I never wanted a bun so badly."

"In the tree house," said Daisy.

Robert turned the boat about and again began pulling for his own shore. He was getting hungrier and hungrier. At last when the boat was halfway across, he lifted his oars and rested them in the locks. "I'm hungry," he said.

"In the tree house," said Daisy, as she saw Robert's eyes on the bag of buns.

"Look," said Robert. "I rowed over for you and then I rowed back and then I rowed over again for the buns and now I'm rowing back. I'm hungry!"

"In the tree house," said Daisy, but her voice sounded a little bit weak.

"I'm going to make believe I'm in the tree house right now and have my bun, and if you don't give it to me we'll just sit here in the middle of the river all day," said Robert.

Daisy handed over the bag and Robert took out a big round currant bun. Then Timothy took his and Jeffrey took his, and Daisy said, "I guess I might as well eat mine." So they all sat in the rowboat eating currant buns.

"I wish I had some milk," said Daisy.

"You can drink your milk in the tree house," said Timothy.

"Well, I'm glad I don't have to row across the river to get it," said Robert as he tied up the boat.

Daisy and the twins ran to the willow tree while Robert went to the house to get the milk. When he returned he found that the others had climbed up the tree to the tree house. "Let the basket down," Robert called up.

Timothy lowered the basket that hung on the end of the rope and Robert placed two milk bottles and four mugs in the basket. "Haul her up!" he cried out.

Timothy began pulling the basket up to the tree house while Jeffrey and Daisy looked down and shouted directions. Robert climbed the ladder and reached the tree house just as Timothy untied the basket.

As Robert poured out the milk, Daisy said, "I wish I had a currant bun."

"In the boat you said you wished you had some milk," said Robert.

"I know," said Daisy. "It's all your fault, Robert, that we don't have any buns to eat with our milk. They were tree-house buns, not rowboat buns."

The boys laughed and Robert poured out more milk into their mugs.

Chapter Two

WHAT ROBERT FOUND

ROBERT awoke early one morning. The house was quiet. Only the sound of a woodpecker working on a tree reached his ears. Even before he got out of bed Robert could tell that it was a misty morning. Odors of herbs from his mother's garden came through his window on the damp air. It would not be a good morning for a swim, but he could take the rowboat out if he kept close to the shore.

It was the kind of morning Robert liked, with the mist lying on the river. It was a morning for finding things along the bank. Because he could not see very far he looked more carefully nearby.

Robert washed and dressed quickly. He tiptoed past his father's and mother's room to the kitchen. He took the box of cornflakes from the kitchen closet and filled a bowl. Then he brought the milk from the refrigerator and poured it over the cornflakes. He listened to them crackle as he sprinkled sugar over them. Then he poured himself a glass of milk and sat down at the kitchen table.

It did not take Robert long to eat his breakfast. He rinsed out his bowl and his glass and left them beside the sink. When his mother saw them she would know that he had gone out.

Robert put on his waterproof, for he knew that the mist would be wet on the river. Then he went out the side door and ran down to the little dock where the boat was tied.

It didn't take long to untie it, and in a minute Robert was in the rowboat, rowing downstream. Mist like ghostly fishnets drifted above the water. Robert kept close to the bank. As it slipped by him, he peered into the reeds and rushes that grew by the river's edge. He was sure that he would find something if he just looked hard enough.

Once he saw a water rat duck into a hole in the bank. He passed under willow trees like his own and heard birds calling to each other. Occasionally he heard the sound of a car or truck passing along the main road that ran parallel to the river, but the mist muffled the sound so that the road seemed farther away than it was.

Before long he reached the banks of Mr. Lovell's place. Mr. Lovell lived alone and built sailboats. Robert looked up at Mr. Lovell's workshop. Three hulls lay upside down beside the shop. They were covered with tarpaulins to protect them. Through the open door, Robert could see a sailboat that was almost finished. He was glad that holiday time was here, for now he would be able to drop by and see how the sailboats were coming along.

Mr. Lovell's house was the last one before some open meadows. Here again trees bordered the river. As Robert passed under the trees, he heard a strange noise overhead. Robert knew most of the bird calls, but this sound was new. It was a chattering sound. Robert looked up. At first he noticed nothing unusual. Then suddenly he saw something that surprised him. Sitting on a branch, halfway up the tree, was a little monkey. At first he could not believe his eyes, for Robert knew that monkeys did not live in the trees along the River Thames. But when it began chattering again and jumping up and down on the branch, he was certain that it was a real, live monkey. Robert looked around, for suddenly he felt that he was in another world. In a jungle! Then, out of the mist that hung over the meadow, a boy about a year or two older than Robert appeared. He was almost as strange a sight as the monkey.

The boy's skin was the color of a chestnut, and his jet-black hair fell over his forehead in thick black curls. As he drew nearer Robert could see that his deep-set eyes were dark blue. He was wearing a pair of old green corduroy trousers, cut off just below his knees. Frayed ends hung like fringe against his dark legs. A bright shirt made of flowered silk, many sizes too large for him, hung outside of his trousers. Knotted around his neck was a brilliant yellow handkerchief. As he stood under the trees, he looked like a bright parrot.

Robert looked at the boy and then up at the monkey. Neither looked real. He rubbed his eyes and looked back at the boy. The boy was still standing in the same spot, his eyes fixed on Robert. Finally Robert spoke. "Do you know, there's a monkey up in this tree!" he said.

"Aow!" cried the boy, and he ran to the water's edge and looked up.

"Where do you suppose it came from?" Robert asked.

"He's mine," was the reply. This was followed by loud shouts. "Come down, Jobi! Come down!"

"You can see him better if you come into the boat," said Robert.

"I ain't never been in a boat," the boy answered.

Robert looked surprised, and said, "Have you just come to live on the river?"

"No. I don't live on the river," the boy answered.

"Well, my name's Robert," said Robert.

"I'm Aaron," the boy replied. Then he looked up in the tree and shouted again to the monkey. Aaron said, "I can't see him."

"Come into the boat. You can see him from here," said Robert.

Aaron looked down at the boat and frowned. "It looks so shaky," he said.

"Oh, not when you get used to it," Robert replied.

"It won't upset, will it?" Aaron asked.

"Not if you sit still," said Robert, holding out his hand.

The boy took hold of Robert's hand and stepped out. "Just be careful," said Robert, but almost before he had finished speaking there was a great splash, and Aaron was in the river up to his neck. Robert grabbed an oar and held it out to him, but Aaron reached for the side of the boat. "Take hold of the oar!" Robert cried. "Don't hold onto the boat, you might upset it."

Aaron clutched the oar. "Don't be afraid," said Robert. "Hold onto the oar and I'll tow you along to that little spot where you can get out on the bank. It isn't very far."

Aaron held tightly to the oar, and in a few moments Robert got the boat to the spot where Aaron could take hold of a fallen tree trunk and pull himself out of the river. His bright clothes were covered with green slime from the weeds that grew under the water. Water ran from his hair, his nose, his chin, from his arms and his hands, and down his legs.

"I'm sorry you got so wet," said Robert. "It's really very simple to get into the boat. If you'll take hold of my hand, we'll try it again."

"No, I've got to get my monkey!" said Aaron, running back to the tree where the monkey was still sitting on the high limb. He seemed to be enjoying the sight below him.

Robert rowed back to the spot where he had first spotted the monkey. The monkey was jumping up and down now, and Aaron was calling, "Come down, Jobi! You good-for-nothing monkey, come down!"

Jobi just chattered and jumped to a higher limb.

"Now I can't see him at all!" cried Aaron.

"I can see him," said Robert, pointing up into the tree. "Come into the boat and you can see him."

Aaron took hold of Robert's hand, and this time he stepped into the boat and sat down. Then he looked up into the tree. He shook his fist at the monkey. "If I just had a banana, he'd come down," said Aaron.

"Well, I think we have some bananas at our house," said Robert. "It's not far. We can be there in a jiffy."

Robert began rowing back to the dock as quickly as he could. Aaron sat facing him, still dripping water. Robert was puzzled by this dark boy in strange clothes who owned a monkey. At last Robert said, "Where do you live?"

"In the wagon," replied Aaron. "My father is helping on a farm. Helping with the vegetables."

"Oh!" exclaimed Robert. "You have a trailer! You hitch it to your car."

"Ours is a wagon with a horse," said Aaron. "We're Romanies."

"Oh!" cried Robert. "You're from Rome! I've been to Rome. I went last year on our holidays. It's in Italy."

"No, no," replied Aaron. "I'm English, like you. People call us Gypsies."

"Oh, Gypsies!" Robert cried, opening his eyes very wide. "I've seen Gypsy wagons. I think they're super!"

"You do?" said Aaron with a smile. "You like wagons?"

"Oh, yes," said Robert.

"Someday my father is going to have a trailer," said Aaron. "He's earning the money to buy one. I guess he'll get it, but I'll be sorry to see the wagon go. And I'll miss the horse."

As Robert pulled the boat to his own dock, he said, "Now, do be very careful getting out. I'll help you."

"It does rock, doesn't it?" said Aaron, grabbing Robert's hand.

When Aaron was safely on the shore, Robert climbed out of the boat. Aaron watched Robert tie up the boat. "Come along," said Robert, leading

Aaron through the garden past the swimming pool and around to the back door of the house.

Robert's mother was in the kitchen when Robert burst in. "Mummy!" he cried. "I've found a new friend! And we have to have a banana. It's for his monkey."

"Monkey!" his mother exclaimed, looking very surprised.

"Yes," said Robert. "You see, this is Aaron." Aaron had hung back. He was standing by a bench and looking down at his feet. Robert turned and called to him. "Come here, Aaron. This is my mother."

Aaron took a few steps nearer the door as Robert's mother came out. "How do you do, Aaron," she said.

"Hello," Aaron murmured, without looking up.

"He lives in a wagon, Mummy," said Robert. "You know, one of those beautiful painted wagons." Turning to Aaron, he said, "It's painted, isn't it?"

Aaron nodded.

"With trimmings?" said Robert.

Aaron nodded again.

"You see, Mummy, he's a Gypsy," said Robert, "and his father is helping a farmer with his vegetables."

"I see," said his mother. "But how did he get so wet?"

"Oh, that's because he fell into the river," said Robert. "He was trying to see the monkey. Can we have a banana for the monkey, please, Mummy?"

"But where is the monkey?" his mother asked.

"It's up in a tree," said Robert.

"Oh, now I understand," said his mother. "But Aaron should take off those wet clothes." Then looking at the green slime that was clinging to him, she added, "And he should have a bath."

Aaron looked startled.

"Oh, we have to get Jobi!" said Robert. "He might get farther away."

Mrs. Spencer went into the kitchen. When she

came back to the boys, she said, "Here, take the banana, and hurry back."

Robert took the banana, and the two boys ran back to the boat. Robert unfastened it and jumped in. "Now take it easy," he said, as he saw Aaron about to step into the boat. This time Aaron got in without any help from Robert.

Robert picked up the oars and set off. The mist was lifting now and a watery sun was beginning to seep through. Soon they reached the big horse-chestnut tree where they had left Jobi. They looked up into the branches, but there was no sign of the monkey. "I don't see him," said Robert.

"Jobi! Jobi!" Aaron shouted. He was answered by the cry of a sea gull over the river.

"He's gone!" said Robert.

"He's hiding," said Aaron. "I know his tricks." Then in a very coaxing tone, Aaron called, "Come, Jobi. Here, Jobi. Come and get the nice banana. Come, Jobi."

All was quiet. Then a bird called from overhead. A motorboat roared by. It was quiet again. "Here, Jobi," Aaron called once more.

The boys waited. Then, from behind the trunk of the horse-chestnut tree, a little face with beady eyes peered out of the undergrowth. Aaron saw him and held up the banana.

The monkey came running on his awkward legs and, when he was near, with one leap landed in the boat. The boys laughed. "He's better at getting into boats than you, Aaron," said Robert.

"That's right," Aaron replied, as he broke the banana in half. He handed a piece of the banana to Robert, and said, "Here. If you feed him, he'll make friends with you."

The monkey sat in the boat and ate the piece of banana that Aaron had given him. Then he reached out quickly and took the piece that Robert held out to him.

Robert watched the monkey as he ate the banana.

Robert had never been so close to a monkey before. He could hardly wait to show it to his mother. And wouldn't the twins be excited! he thought to himself. And Daisy! Daisy would probably be afraid of the monkey. As the last bit of banana disappeared into the monkey's mouth, Robert said, "I'm hungry too! Let's go back. I want Mummy to see Jobi."

Aaron shook his head. "I have to go now," he said.

"But you could go swimming in our pool," said Robert. "I've got some swimming trunks that are big enough for you. Then your clothes could dry."

"Thanks," said Aaron, but he shook his head.

"You could stay for lunch," said Robert. "We could eat it in the tree house."

Aaron shook his head again.

"You'd like the tree house," said Robert, "but if you didn't, we could have it on the porch."

"I've got to go back," said Aaron.

"Or in our other boat. In the motorboat," said Robert. "Often I have my lunch in the motorboat or

in my tent. I sleep in the tent almost every night. I guess I'm sort of a Gypsy, just like you."

Aaron smiled, and his teeth looked very white in his dark face.

"Maybe you could come and sleep in my tent with me some night," said Robert. "There's plenty of room."

"Thanks," said Aaron, as he placed Jobi on the shore.

Robert saw that Aaron was leaving him, so he said, "Be careful! Don't dunk yourself again."

Aaron was careful as he climbed out of the boat. He picked up his monkey, and said, "Thanks for the banana." Robert watched him walk away through the field. The sun was out now and patches of sunlight lay on the ground.

Aaron turned and looked back at Robert. Robert waved his hand and called to him. "Come again!" he shouted.

Aaron waved, but he did not call out. Now, in the

sunlight, his clothes looked brighter than ever. He looked even more like a parrot than he had when he first appeared.

Robert took up his oars, and as he rowed home he began to wonder whether Aaron and the monkey were real, or whether he had fallen asleep in the boat and dreamed that he had seen a monkey in a tree and a Gypsy boy.

That night, when he told his father about his morning adventure, Robert said, "I never thought I would ever find a monkey on the river."

"Or a Gypsy boy! Gypsies are almost as scarce as monkeys today," said his father. "By the way, do you call them 'all sorts'?"

"Oh, no," replied Robert. "They're not 'all sorts.' They're my friends." Then he added, "I do hope they will come back."

Chapter Three

AARON AND THE SWAN

Robert could hardly wait to tell Daisy and the twins about Aaron and Jobi. The very next morning he set out for the opposite shore in the rowboat. As he was tying up the boat, Daisy called to him from the towpath, "Hello, Robby! Are we going over to the tree house? I could bring some more currant buns."

Robert brushed the currant buns aside, and said, "I've got some very exciting news."

"What kind of news?" Daisy asked.

"Come along to the twins' and I'll tell you," said Robert.

Daisy ran beside Robert. She was a very little girl, although she was the same age as Robert. But in spite of the fact that her legs were short, she could always keep up with Robert and the twins. When Daisy and Robert reached the twins' house, they found Timothy and Jeffrey riding their bicycles around their driveway. As soon as Daisy saw them, she called out, "Robby's got some exciting news!"

"What is it?" said the twins in one voice, as they got off their bicycles.

Robert felt very important as the three children stood waiting for him to speak. Then he said, "You'll never guess what I found down the river yesterday."

"What?" said the children in a chorus.

"A monkey!" said Robert.

There was a moment's silence, then Daisy spoke. "I don't believe you. You're making it up."

"I am not," said Robert.

"Where was this monkey?" said Timothy.

"Up in a tree," replied Robert.

"You just thought you saw a monkey," said Jeffrey. "There are no monkeys on the Thames."

"I know a monkey when I see one," said Robert. "It was in my boat, too, and I fed it part of a banana."

"Oh, Robby. How can you say such things?" said Daisy.

"And there was Aaron, too," said Robert.

"Aaron!" said Daisy. "What's an Aaron?"

"Not an Aaron," said Robert. "Aaron. Jobi belongs to Aaron."

"Who is Jobi?" Timothy asked.

"The monkey, of course," said Robert. "And Aaron is my friend. And do you know something?"

"What?" said the three children.

"He's a Gypsy," replied Robert.

Daisy let out a squeal. "A Gypsy!" she cried, in an awestruck voice. "Oh, not a Gypsy!"

"Yes," said Robert. "He's very nice, too. He lives in one of those beautiful wagons with a horse. His father is helping on a farm."

Timothy ignored this news. "What happened to the monkey?" he asked.

"Nothing happened to it," Robert replied. "You see, it had run away and got up in the tree. Aaron was looking for it, and then he fell into the river. The monkey came down for the banana, and then Aaron took the monkey home."

"You're making this all up," said Daisy.

"I'll take you to the very spot where I saw it," said Robert.

The twins dropped their bicycles right on the drive and started for the dock.

"You coming, Daisy?" Robert asked.

"I don't like monkeys, and I'm not allowed to go near Gypsies. They steal. They even steal children." She leaned toward Robert, and said with a mysterious air, "A Gypsy woman came to our door when I was a tiny baby. She was selling clothespins, but she was really looking for babies to steal."

"Now who's makings things up?" said Timothy, who had come back to see what was keeping Robert. "Come on, Daisy. Nobody is going to steal you. We're just going to see if the monkey has come back to that tree. Come on."

Daisy followed the boys to the boat. Jeffrey was already seated in the stern. Timothy and Robert jumped in. Daisy stood on the dock uncertainly.

"If you're not coming, Daisy," said Robert, "I'm going to untie the boat."

"I'll come," she said, and stepped in. Daisy sat down and Robert untied the rope. Then he picked up the oars and began to row across. When he reached the other side he turned downriver, keeping close to the shore. It was not long before he came to the spot where he had found Jobi and Aaron.

Robert pointed to the tree, and said, "It was right here that I saw the monkey—Jobi."

Timothy, Jeffrey, and Daisy all looked up into the tree. "He isn't there now," said Timothy.

"Well, I guess he doesn't run away every day," said Robert.

"I wish I could see him," said Jeffrey. "I like monkeys."

"There's nobody around here," said Daisy.

Robert took up his oars. "Let's go downriver a little bit," he said.

There was a bend in the river just ahead, and as the boat rounded the bend Jeffrey, who was seated in the stern, called out, "Oh, Robby! Look!"

"Oh, yes," Timothy cried, "look!"

Robert and Daisy both looked toward the shore. "Oh!" Daisy cried. "It's them! It's them!"

"It's Aaron," said Robert. "He's fishing."

"He's got the monkey with him!" Daisy cried. "Let's go home! Robby, let's go home!"

"No! Let's go see the monkey," said Timothy.

"That's what we came for," said Jeffrey.

"But I didn't think it was real," Daisy cried. "I really didn't."

Meanwhile, Robert was rowing nearer to the spot where Aaron was fishing. "Oh! You won't let that monkey in the boat, will you?" said Daisy. "Monkeys have lice on them. I don't want to get lice on me."

"Hi, Aaron!" Robert called out. "Are you catching anything?" He rested his oars beside the bank. "I've brought my friends this morning," he added.

"Oh, Robby," Daisy whispered, "don't go too near. The monkey might jump into the boat."

"How's Jobi?" Robert called to Aaron.

Aaron paid no attention to Robert. He was tugging at his fishing line, waving and snapping the pole and pulling with all of his strength.

"What's the matter with your pole?" Robert called.

Aaron pointed out into the river in the direction of his fishing line. "You see that swan out there?" he called.

The children looked. "Yes," said Robert.

"That swan has got my hook and he won't let go."
Aaron tugged on the line, and said, "But I'm going
to make him let go. I'll pull his head off. This is my
new pole."

The children's mouths dropped open in horror.
Daisy covered her face with her hands.

"Oh, no!" cried Robert. "Don't! It can't let go.
The hook is caught in its beak or maybe in its
throat!"

"If that's one of the Queen's swans, they'll take
you right to the Tower of London and chop off your
head," said Jeffrey, who usually made things seem as
bad as possible.

Aaron stopped tugging on the line. He no longer
looked angry. Instead, his face was filled with fear.

"We'll have to get the Queen's Swankeeper," said
Robert, "that's what we'll have to do."

"Oh!" cried Aaron. "The police are always making trouble for us Romanies."

"He isn't the police," said Robert. "He'll just come

and get the hook out of the swan's beak. He knows how to do it. I'll row back and ask Mummy to call him on the telephone."

"What shall I do?" asked Aaron.

"You hold the line until the Swankeeper comes," said Robert. "If you drop it, that swan may trail the line around the river for days before the Swankeeper can find it."

"I hope the hook isn't in the swan's throat," said Jeffrey, as Robert picked up his oars. Robert turned the boat around and started rowing for his own dock.

"That Gypsy won't be there when the Swankeeper comes," said Timothy, as Robert pulled hard on the oars.

"He'll drop his pole and run," said Jeffrey.

"Did you see how scared he looked when you said you would tell the Queen's Swankeeper?" said Daisy.

"The Swankeeper will never see that Gypsy," said Timothy.

"How do you know he won't?" said Robert.

"Because Gypsies steal and cheat," said Jeffrey.

"How many Gypsies do you know?" Robert asked.

Jeffrey could not speak for a moment. Then he said, "Well, I don't know any, but I've heard plenty about them."

"Huh," said Robert, "you don't know any. Well, I know one and he's a friend of mine, and he doesn't cheat or steal."

"How long have you known him?" said Timothy.

"Ever since yesterday," replied Robert.

"Ha, ha, ha!" Jeffrey laughed. "Since yesterday!"

Daisy and Timothy joined in the laughter, "Ha, ha, ha!"

"Just wait and see," said Daisy, as Robert brought the boat to the dock.

The children scrambled out and Robert made the boat fast. Then he ran to the house and shouted to his mother, who was in the kitchen. "Call up the Queen's Swankeeper, Mummy! A swan has its beak caught on Aaron's fishhook. He's downriver in the field below Mr. Lovell's place."

Robert's mother went to the telephone and dialed the number for the Queen's Swankeeper. Robert stood beside his mother and listened while she spoke to the Swankeeper. When she hung up, she said, "He'll go right down and find Aaron and the swan."

"Aaron will wait, won't he, Mummy?" said Robert.

"I certainly hope so," his mother replied. "It's dreadful for the swan when people drop their lines, and it's hard for the Swankeeper to find it."

Robert clenched his fists, and said, "But Aaron won't do that. I know he won't." Then with less force he said, "Well, anyway, I don't think he will." He looked into his mother's face. There were tears in his eyes. "You don't think he will leave that swan, do you, Mummy?"

His mother put her arm around him, and said, "What would you do, Robert?"

"I'd wait," said Robert.

"Of course you would," said his mother. "Now trust Aaron to do what you would do."

Robert ran back to his friends on the dock. "The Swankeeper is going right away," he said.

"He won't find that Gypsy," said Jeffrey.

Robert made no reply. Instead, he went to the row-boat, and said, "Come on, everybody. It's lunchtime. I have to take you home."

Robert was only halfway across the river when the boat of the Queen's Swankeeper passed. The children waved to him, and the Swankeeper shouted, "Hello!" The children watched him as he sped down the river to the field where they had left Aaron.

Chapter Four

TO THE RESCUE

WHEN the boat rounded the bend of the river and came toward Aaron, he knew at once that it was the Queen's Swankeeper, for he was wearing a blue coat and a hat trimmed with gold braid.

The Swankeeper shut off his motor, and called to Aaron, "I'll have your line free in a few minutes. You did the right thing holding on to your rod."

Then the Swankeeper picked up the oars that were in the boat and Aaron watched him row out into the middle of the river where the swan was floating. The awful worry that had been making Aaron unhappy left him. He wasn't in trouble after all. The man had not even scolded him. He wished that he could watch the Swankeeper remove the hook, but he was too far away to see that. He did see the swan beat its wings as the Swankeeper took hold of it. Before long Aaron felt his line free. He reeled it in. The Swankeeper waved his hand as he turned and started back up the river.

Aaron watched the swan swim to the opposite bank. With a sense of relief, he lay down on the grass. Jobi squatted beside him. Aaron was glad he still had his fishing rod. The warm sun beating down upon him made him sleepy. Soon he was fast asleep, with Jobi curled up beside him.

Aaron woke up sometime later, hearing someone calling him. He sat up and looked around. For a moment he did not know where he was, but then he saw Robert coming toward him. Robert was carrying a basket. "I thought you would be here," said Robert as he came near. "Mummy packed a lunch for us."

Aaron jumped up. "Where are your friends?" he asked, as Robert put down the basket.

"Oh, I took them across the river," Robert replied. "They had to go home for their lunch."

Jobi was jumping around, trying to open the basket. Aaron gave him a little slap. "Git!" he said.

"I've brought Jobi a banana," said Robert.

"He'll like that," said Aaron, sitting down again. "Give it to him, and he'll leave us alone."

Robert opened the basket and took out the banana. When he held it out Jobi grabbed it. Then he jumped up and down with delight. Finally he ran off a little way and began to peel the banana.

Robert took out two bottles of orange drink and handed one to Aaron. Then he handed Aaron a sandwich. "There are plenty of these," he said. "And there's cherry cake. Do you like cherry cake?"

"I never had it," Aaron replied, "but I'll like it, all right. I like everything to eat. I never had a lunch packed up like this before." Then he looked up at Robert, and said, "Your mam's nice." Aaron took a large bite out of his sandwich, and when he could speak again, he said, "That girl was afraid, wasn't she?"

"You mean Daisy?" Robert asked. "You mustn't mind Daisy. She never saw a monkey outside of a zoo before."

Aaron was not fooled by Robert's half answer. As he took another sandwich from Robert's hand, he said, "People run away from us Romanies. They look strange looks at me. Sometimes they call out, 'Gyppo! Gyppo!'"

"You mustn't pay any attention to them," said Robert. "They don't have any manners, that's what's the matter with them." He bit into an apple.

"What do you mean, manners?" Aaron asked.

Robert took another bite of apple while he thought

about how to answer Aaron's question. At last he said, "Well, I guess it's making people feel good instead of making people feel bad."

"I guess I don't have any," said Aaron, "because I don't like the Gaujos and I want to make them feel bad."

"What are the Gaujos?" asked Robert.

"Anybody who isn't a Romany," Aaron replied, "and I make them feel bad, because they make me feel bad." Then he looked sideways at Robert, and said, "But you don't make me feel bad."

"That's because we're friends," said Robert, handing Aaron an apple.

"Did you hear anything about that swan?" Aaron asked, changing the subject.

"Yes," replied Robert. "Mummy talked to the Swankeeper. The hook was just in its beak, not in its throat. So that was good."

"Did it belong to the Queen?" Aaron asked.

"Yes, it did," said Robert. "It didn't have any mark

on its beak. When they don't have any mark, they belong to the Queen."

Aaron looked uneasy and rubbed his neck.

Robert laughed. "Oh, the Queen wouldn't chop your head off," he said. "Jeffrey just says things like that. He likes to make a big fuss."

"Well, maybe the Queen wouldn't, but if I had dropped my new fishing pole in the river my father would have chopped off my head, and it wouldn't have been the first time, either."

Robert laughed and laughed. "How can you have your head chopped off more than once?" he shouted.

When all of the sandwiches and all of the cherry cake and the apples had disappeared, Robert put the empty bottles back into the basket. "I tied the boat up to Mr. Lovell's dock," he said. "Come walk back with me."

Aaron got up, picked up Jobi, and walked to the dock with Robert. "Come, get in the boat," said Robert. "We'll take Jobi for a ride."

"Oh, he'll like that," said Aaron, as Robert helped him into the boat. Robert placed the picnic basket on the bottom of the boat beside Aaron and picked up the oars. He had not rowed very far from the dock when Mr. Lovell appeared.

"Hi, Mr. Lovell!" Robert called out. "How's the new sailboat?"

"Hello, Bob-o-Link!" Mr. Lovell replied. "It's finished. Come on back and see it."

Robert turned the rowboat around and rowed back to the dock. Mr. Lovell tied the boat and the boys got out. "This is my friend Aaron, Mr. Lovell," said Robert, "and this is his monkey Jobi."

Mr. Lovell held out his hand to Aaron, and said, "How do you do."

Aaron wiped his hands on his trousers and took hold of Mr. Lovell's hand. He didn't say anything. Instead he bowed the way he had seen his father bow to an old gentleman that his father always called the Rai.

"Come into the workshop," said Mr. Lovell.

"I'm glad Aaron can see your new sailboat," said Robert, as the two boys followed Mr. Lovell. As he opened the door the mingled odor of wood, paint, and varnish was very strong. The sailboat was resting in a wooden cradle.

"I've just sold the boat to a man from London," said Mr. Lovell.

"It's a great sailboat," said Robert.

Aaron stood looking around the shop at the boat and at the wood piled up on a table and the pieces of wood that lay on the floor.

Robert walked all around the boat, admiring it. He looked at the stern, and said, "Why doesn't it have a name painted on it?"

"The man who bought it hasn't decided upon a name," replied Mr. Lovell.

Aaron had been so interested in looking around the shop that he hadn't noticed that Jobi had disappeared. Suddenly there was a terrible bang. Something had fallen. This noise was followed by more bangs and a rattling of cans.

Mr. Lovell and the boys ran to the back of the shop. There was Jobi on a shelf, knocking cans of paint down to the floor below him. Even worse, he had put his foot into an open can of blue paint. When he saw Mr. Lovell coming toward him, he let out a cry of glee and kicked the can off the shelf. Paint splashed out of the can as it fell to the floor and Jobi, with a bright blue foot and leg, jumped down after it. He landed in a puddle of paint.

Aaron rushed to pick him up, but before he could catch him Jobi flew to the sailboat. He jumped up on the deck with its pure white coat of paint, leaving blue footprints wherever he stepped. "Jobi! Jobi! Jobi!" Aaron shouted, as he ran after his monkey.

Mr. Lovell tried to grab the monkey, but Aaron cried out, "Don't touch him, Rai! I'll get him! He's used to me."

Jobi jumped down into the bottom of the boat and

hid under the deck, but Aaron wasn't afraid of him. He jumped in after Jobi, reached right under the deck, and pulled the monkey out. Then, as quick as lightning, Aaron ran out of the shop and toward the open field.

Robert and Mr. Lovell watched in surprise. Then they ran out after him. They found him right away, for Jobi had set up a shrill cry. Aaron was behind a bush, shaking with fright, and Jobi's arms were around his neck. As Mr. Lovell bent over him, Aaron crouched down. He turned his head away as far as he could and put his arms up to ward off a blow. But Mr. Lovell did not strike him. Instead Mr. Lovell said, "Aaron, get up at once. Bring the monkey back. We must get that paint off him. It may poison him. Do you want your monkey to die?"

"Oh, no! Oh, no!" cried Aaron, getting to his feet.

"Then bring him right back to the sink," said Mr. Lovell.

Aaron carried the crying monkey back into the

workshop, and Mr. Lovell led the way to the sink. He picked up a bottle of turpentine from the paint shelf as he went by.

Aaron held Jobi in the sink. The monkey was screaming now. "It won't kill him, will it, Rai?" Aaron asked.

"We'll have to work fast," said Mr. Lovell. "You should not have run away."

Robert wished that he could do more than hold the can of turpentine. He also wished that Jobi would stop screeching.

Mr. Lovell had a lot of old rags, and he used them to wipe the monkey's legs until the rags no longer showed any blue.

"What about the boat, Rai?" Aaron asked, as he lifted Jobi out of the sink. "Jobi spoiled your boat."

"I think I can get those marks off with turpentine, but if I can't I'll have to repaint it."

"He's a wicked monkey," said Aaron, "and I'm sorry. I guess I shouldn't have come here."

"That's foolish talk," said Mr. Lovell. "You can come whenever you want."

"I'll leave Jobi home," said Aaron.

"No," said Mr. Lovell, laughing, "you wouldn't look natural without Jobi. Just keep your eye on him the next time you come."

Robert moved toward the door, and said, "I guess I'd better be getting back home."

"I'll get to work on my boat," said Mr. Lovell.

"Do you mind if I stay and watch you?" Aaron asked. "I want to see if you can get that paint off."

"Certainly, you can stay," said Mr. Lovell.

"I'll hold on to Jobi," said Aaron.

Robert called good-bye, and Mr. Lovell and Aaron waved to him as he went out the door.

While Mr. Lovell was getting a clean rag and his can of turpentine, Aaron picked up a small piece of wood from the floor. "Rai," said Aaron, "could I have this piece of wood to whittle?"

"Take it along," replied Mr. Lovell, beginning to remove a blue spot from the deck of the boat.

Aaron watched. "Is it coming off, Rai?" he asked.

"I think it is," replied Mr. Lovell.

"I'm glad!" said Aaron.

Mr. Lovell scrubbed at the spots. After a while he said, "Aaron, what is this name that you call me— Rai?"

"It's Romany language," said Aaron. "It means gentleman."

Mr. Lovell looked up at Aaron, and said, "That's very nice, Aaron. Thank you. I hope you will always call me that."

After some time Mr. Lovell looked the boat over, and said, "Well! I believe I've got all of that blue paint off."

"That's good," said Aaron. "I'll go now. You were good to Jobi, Rai."

Mr. Lovell said good-bye to Aaron at the door, and then he turned back and looked at the sailboat. "Glad I got that paint off," he said to himself.

But he had forgotten that Jobi had hidden under the deck.

Chapter Five

MR. LOVELL'S SAILBOAT

O<small>NE</small> afternoon Daisy and the twins were sitting with Robert beside the Spencers' swimming pool, when Jeffrey said, "Say, Robby. What happened about the swan that Gyppo hooked?"

"The Swankeeper took the hook out of the swan's beak, and it was all right," Robert replied.

"I'll bet the Gyppo wasn't there when the Swan-keeper got there," said Jeffrey.

"Aaron was so there," said Robert, "and he's no Gyppo!"

"Course he's a Gyppo," said Jeffrey. "He's a Gypsy, isn't he?"

"Yes, he's a Gypsy," said Robert. "There isn't anything the matter with being a Gypsy."

"Yes, there is," said Timothy. "They live in wagons."

"Well, I like wagons," said Robert. "I wish I had one of those Gypsy wagons."

"They sleep in tents," said Daisy. "They don't sleep in beds."

"Well, I sleep in a tent," said Robert. He pointed to the other side of the garden, and said, "And it's right over there."

The three children looked across at the tent. They were quiet for a few moments. Then Jeffrey said, "Gyppos can't read or write. They're ignorant."

"Well, Aaron can read and write," said Robert. "I know he can."

"How do you know he can?" Jeffrey asked.

"Because he's bigger than I am," said Robert. "He's older, and everybody older than I am can read and write."

Jeffrey laughed. "Bet you he can't," he said.

Timothy got up. "Last one in the pool is a Gyppo!" he said.

Daisy, Jeffrey, and Timothy started to run to the pool, but Robert called out, "No! It's time for me to row you over to the other side."

The children stood still. "You mean it's time for us to go home?" Timothy asked.

"Yes," replied Robert.

Jeffrey looked up at the sun, and said, "But it's early! We don't have to go home yet."

"I have something I want to do," said Robert. "If you want me to take you across the river, you'll have to come now."

While the children dressed, no one said a word. As they walked to the dock, Timothy whispered to Jeffrey, "If you hadn't started that Gyppo business, we could have had some more fun in the pool."

"Well, you did it too," said Jeffrey.

"You started it," said Timothy.

The children were very quiet as Robert rowed them across the river. When they reached the other side, Daisy was the first to step out of the boat. "Thanks, Robby," she said. "I had a very nice time."

When Timothy got out, he said, "It was fun swimming, Robby, and thanks for coming over for us."

"I'll come over again someday," said Robert, but he didn't sound as though it would be soon.

"Well, then, I'll bring the currant buns," said Daisy, trying to make everyone feel better.

As Jeffrey climbed onto the dock, he said, "I'd like to see that monkey again someday."

"Well, maybe," said Robert, as he swung his boat around.

As Robert pulled out into the river, Timothy gave Jeffrey a poke with his elbow, and said, "Why didn't you say you were sorry about that Gyppo business?"

Jeffrey just shrugged his shoulders.

As Robert rowed back he thought of Aaron. He had not seen Aaron since the day the swan got hooked on his line. He wondered whether Aaron had gone away. It would be terrible if Aaron had left, thought Robert, before he had even seen the Gypsy wagon!

Robert decided to set out to find the wagon. He did not know where it was, but he was certain it could not be far away. As soon as he had tied up the boat, Robert ran to the garage where he kept his bicycle. He wheeled it out through the gate, and in a few minutes he was pedaling along the highway.

On the river side of the road there were houses that faced the water. Occasionally there was an open field. On the other side of the road there were big fields where farmers were growing vegetables. There were fields of beans, of Brussels sprouts, of cabbages, onions, and potatoes, all ripe now for picking. Robert felt that the Gypsy wagon would be on that side of the road, so he kept a sharp lookout.

Not far along the way Robert came to a gasoline station and a small grocery store. The store also sold candy, and as Robert had a few pennies in his pocket, he decided to go in and buy some gumdrops. Robert knew the store well, for his mother often sent him on his bicycle to buy groceries there.

As he opened the door Mr. Grimes, who owned the store, said, "Well, Robert! What can I do for you?"

"I'd like a package of gumdrops, please," said Robert.

As Mr. Grimes reached into the case for the gum-drops, he said, "And how are you enjoying your days, now that you don't have to go to school?"

"Oh, I'm having a lot of fun," replied Robert. Then as Mr. Grimes handed him the gumdrops, Robert said, "You don't happen to know where there is a Gypsy wagon, do you? It's around here some-where."

"A Gypsy wagon!" said Mr. Grimes, as he took Robert's pennies. "Seems to me there's one not too far up the road, pulled into the woods." Then Mr. Grimes looked very troubled, and said, "I don't think you ought to go there alone, though. Never can tell about Gypsies. Queer lot, I always say."

"Oh, I like Gypsy wagons," said Robert. "I wish I could have one."

Then Mr. Grimes changed the subject with some shocking news. "Have you seen the local paper that just came out today?" he asked. "Big headline about Mr. Lovell's new boat." Mr. Grimes picked up a copy of the newspaper.

"What about the boat?" Robert asked.

Mr. Grimes leaned over the counter and looked right into Robert's face. "Stolen!" he said.

"Do you mean Mr. Lovell's new sailboat that he just made?" asked Robert.

"That's it!" replied Mr. Grimes. "He'd sold it to a man from London." Mr. Grimes slapped the paper, and said, "It's all right here."

At that moment a horn sounded outside. Mr. Grimes handed the paper to Robert, and said, "I have to tend the gas pump now. You can read the paper for yourself. Take it along. I've finished with it."

Robert took the paper, and said, "Thanks, Mr. Grimes."

As Robert picked up his bicycle, Mr. Grimes called to him, "Take my advice and stay away from those Gypsies."

Robert made no reply. He got on his bicycle and continued on his way. He had pedaled about a mile when he rounded a bend in the road. A woods lay ahead. As he drew nearer Robert saw a bright blue wagon that had been drawn off the road and into the woods. The sun shining through the leaves of the trees made bright patches on the wagon as blue as the sky.

Robert crossed the road and got off his bicycle. As he wheeled it toward the wagon he heard the music of a violin. He stopped beneath the trees to listen. The sound did not come from the wagon but from deeper in the woods. As Robert listened he thought the music was beautiful, but it made him feel sad. He wondered who could be playing a violin in the woods. Suddenly the music changed. Now it was wild and gay.

While Robert listened to the music he looked at the wagon. Two windows on the side of it dazzled his eyes, for they shone like pure gold, reflecting the sun. The wagon shafts had been let down to the ground and underbrush was growing up around them.

Robert stood still and looked at Aaron's home, for he was certain this was Aaron's wagon. The door above the shafts was open, and a short flight of removable steps led up to the entrance. A curved canopy over the door was supported by brackets made of wood, carved in beautiful designs. There were carvings over the doorway and down the sides of the door. They were painted in bright colors. Robert had never seen such a gay doorway before. It seemed to say, "Come in!"

Robert leaned his bicycle against a tree. Now the music was coming nearer and nearer. He stood still with his gaze fixed on the woods beyond the wagon. Someone was coming, and, whoever it was, he was making gay music. In a few moments Aaron appeared, playing the violin! When Aaron saw Robert, he stopped playing and lowered his violin. Then he ran toward Robert. Jobi ran beside him. "Robert!" Aaron cried.

"Hi, Aaron!" Robert replied. "Where have you been? I haven't seen you for a long time. That was nice music."

Aaron answered with a bright smile.

"I didn't know you could play the violin." Robert's face was full of admiration.

"It's my dadda's fiddle," said Aaron. "And it was

my granddadda's before. There's a box to keep it in. If you want, I'll show it to you. It's in the *vardo*."

"What's the *vardo?*" Robert asked.

"That's the Romany word for wagon," Aaron replied.

"It's a beautiful wagon," said Robert.

"You like it?" said Aaron, looking very pleased.

"I think it's super," said Robert. "All those trimmings! They're great."

"Come see inside," said Aaron, leading the way to the steps.

Robert followed Aaron. When he stepped inside the wagon, Robert thought he had never seen such a cozy place before. Right beside the door was a little stove. There was no heat coming from it, because the day was heavy with summer heat, but the stove was shiny bright. Across the end of the wagon was a big bed covered with a gay bedspread. A bright rug lay on the floor and white ruffled curtains were at the windows. There was a large painted chest, and above it some hanging shelves that held cups and saucers as well as plates.

Aaron pointed with his bow to a teakettle that stood on the top shelf, and said, "That's my mam's teakettle. It's real silver."

"It's a nice kettle," said Robert.

"It was my grandmam's," said Aaron.

Aaron walked over to the chest and laid his violin and bow on top of it. Then he picked up an old violin case that had once been covered with black leather, but had peeled down to a crumbly brown surface. "This is my granddadda's fiddle box," said Aaron. "Wait till you see inside!" Aaron lifted the lid as though he were about to uncover the Queen's jewels.

Robert looked at the velvety interior. It was faded to the color of dried violets. Aaron picked up the violin. As he was placing it in the case, Robert said, "I wish I could play the violin."

"Oh, you could play it," said Aaron. "You could play it easy."

"I could?" said Robert.

"Sure," said Aaron, as he closed the lid of the violin case. "It just takes a little while."

Suddenly Robert remembered the newspaper that Mr. Grimes had given him. He had been so interested in the wagon and the violin that he had forgotten all about Mr. Lovell's boat. Now he held up the crumpled newspaper that he had been holding in his hand, and said, "Do you know what? Somebody stole Mr. Lovell's sailboat that he just made."

"Stole it!" Aaron exclaimed.

"That's right," said Robert. "It's all in this paper." He knelt down on the floor and spread the paper out in front of him. "It's right here on the front page," he said. "Mr. Grimes showed it to me."

Aaron stood looking down at Robert. Robert looked up, and said, "See, Aaron. It's right here in big letters." Robert began to read, " 'Another theft on the river! New sailboat—' " He hesitated and

pointed to the word *filched*. "What's that word, Aaron?" he said.

"I don't know," Aaron replied. "I can't read."

Robert looked up again, and said, "What do you mean, you can't read? They teach you to read in school, don't they?"

"I don't go to school," said Aaron.

Robert sat back on the floor and stretched his legs out in front of him. He looked at Aaron in amazement. "You don't go to school?" he said.

"No," replied Aaron.

"Never?" Robert asked.

Aaron shook his head.

"But everybody goes to school," said Robert.

"Not Romanies," said Aaron.

"Why not?" Robert exclaimed.

"We travel," said Aaron. "We go all around. Come February we'll leave here and work our way down to Cornwall, where my father works in the daffodil fields."

"But you have to learn to read," said Robert.

"Why?" said Aaron.

"So you can read books," said Robert.

"What's in books?" Aaron asked.

"Oh, all kinds of things. They tell you about everything in the whole world. They tell you wonderful stories."

"Stories!" exclaimed Aaron. "You mean about witches and fairies and hobgoblins and things like that?" Aaron's eyes had grown very big.

"Oh, yes," said Robert.

"My grandmam used to tell me stories," said Aaron.

"They're all in books," said Robert.

"Well, maybe I'd like to read," said Aaron. "Is it hard to learn?"

Robert thought for a few moments, and then he said, "I'll tell you what, Aaron! I'll teach you to read, and you teach me how to play the violin. How about it?"

"Oh, good!" said Aaron with a bright smile.

"Will you come to my house or should I come here?" Robert asked.

"Let's meet in our field on the river," Aaron replied.

"Okay," said Robert. "I'll bring the books and you bring the violin."

As Robert rode home on his bicycle, it seemed to him that teaching Aaron to read and learning to play the violin himself would be very easy. He thought that by next week he would be playing the violin and Aaron would be reading a book. "Then won't I have something to tell the twins and Daisy!" he said, right out loud. He put his hand in his pocket and felt the gumdrops. He had forgotten all about them. "I'll keep them until tomorrow," he said, "and share them with Aaron."

Chapter Six

A RIVER LION

THE following morning Robert carried a whole pile of books from his house to the dock. He placed them in the rowboat. It was still very early, so Robert decided to call on Mr. Lovell before going to meet Aaron. He wanted to ask Mr. Lovell about the sailboat and how it had been stolen.

It was a clear day and the river sparkled in the morning sun. Robert rowed with full deep strokes until he reached Mr. Lovell's dock. There he lifted his oars and laid them in the boat. He fastened it to a ring in the dock and jumped out. Then he ran along the dock to the small gate and lifted the latch. Robert made his way to the door of the workshop, but he found it locked. He decided that Mr. Lovell must be in the house, so he walked along the path that led from the shop to the kitchen door.

When Mr. Lovell came to the door, he said, "Hello there, Bob-o-Link! You're up early. Come in and have some breakfast with me."

"Thanks, Mr. Lovell," said Robert, as he stepped into the kitchen. "I've had my breakfast."

"No room for a buttered sweet roll?"

"Well, maybe a little one," said Robert, sitting down at the table opposite Mr. Lovell. As Mr. Lovell buttered the roll, Robert said, "I'm awfully sorry about your new sailboat."

"Thanks," said Mr. Lovell. "The river police are working on it. I'm hoping they will find it."

"How was it stolen?" Robert asked.

"I left it inside my front gate, and the gate was locked. The thief must have climbed over the wall and unlocked the gate. Then he must have loaded the boat onto the top of a car."

"Maybe the man from London came and got it," said Robert.

"No—he came for the boat later, and we discovered then that it was gone."

"It's mysterious, isn't it?" said Robert.

"It is indeed," replied Mr. Lovell.

The two munched their buns in silence for a few moments. Then Mr. Lovell said, "Well, what are you going to do today, Bob-o-Link?"

"I'm going to learn to play the violin," said Robert.

Mr. Lovell sat up and looked very surprised. "Not all in one day!"

"Well, no," said Robert. "I guess it will take several days, but Aaron says it's easy."

"Oh, Aaron plays the violin, does he?" said Mr. Lovell.

"He plays it very well," replied Robert, "but if you promise not to tell the twins or Daisy, I'll tell you a secret."

"Wouldn't think of it!" said Mr. Lovell. "Never tell secrets."

"Aaron can't read," said Robert. He waited for Mr. Lovell to get the full meaning of this information, then he said, "And he never went to school! Never in his whole life!"

"Gracious!" exclaimed Mr. Lovell, shaking his head. "That's terrible, isn't it?" Then a wide grin spread over Mr. Lovell's face, and he said, "Must be fun, though!"

Robert giggled. "That's what I think too, but I guess it's wrong to think it, because everybody should go to school. You have to learn to read, so you can find out about everything. Why, Mr. Lovell! Aaron couldn't even read what the paper said about your sailboat. Imagine that!"

"Imagine," Mr. Lovell echoed. "I'm glad he can play the violin."

"Well, Aaron's going to teach me to play the violin, and I'm going to teach him to read," said Robert. "Then the twins won't call him a Gyppo."

"They'd better not call him a Gyppo around here," said Mr. Lovell, "or I'll Gyppo the seat of their pants."

Robert laughed again. "I'm going to meet Aaron down in the field after a while," he said. "If you hear anything it will be me learning to play the violin."

Mr. Lovell laughed, and said, "I think I shall enjoy hearing Aaron learning to read more than I'll enjoy hearing you learning to play the violin."

Robert thought this remark was funny. "Well," he

said, "I'll be going along now. Thanks for the nice breakfast."

"Good luck," said Mr. Lovell. "You're going to have a busy day, I can see that."

Robert ran back to his rowboat. He unfastened it and jumped in. He picked up the oars and started downriver. There was plenty of time to do a little treasure hunting before he met Aaron.

Robert had not rowed far when he saw a thick piece of wood floating in the water. He decided at once to find out what it was. He rowed out to where it was floating and, after several attempts, he brought the boat alongside the piece of wood. Robert looked at it carefully and saw that there was more to it than appeared on the surface of the water. He peered down and, to his great surprise, looking back at him was something that seemed to be the face of a small lion. Robert could hardly believe his eyes. Remembering the morning he had found Jobi in a tree, he thought to himself, This is beginning to be a mighty strange river, with monkeys in trees and lions in the water. Robert rested his oar and reached out to touch the surface of the piece of wood. As he pressed his hand on it, the lion's head popped up out of the water. Robert saw that it was a carved wooden lion, seated on the block of wood that he had first seen floating. The lion's paws were holding a shield that rested between its legs.

Robert leaned over the side of the boat and took hold of the base of the figure. He tried to lift it into the boat, but it was too heavy. Robert was afraid that he would upset the boat if he tried to pull the lion over the side. He wondered what he should do. He could not leave this wonderful treasure to float on down the river, but how could he get it into the boat? Robert looked around the bottom of the boat. There he saw a piece of rope. He picked up the rope and reached for the lion's paws. He was so excited he could hardly tie the rope into a knot, but after several attempts he succeeded. Now he was ready to tow his treasure. He picked up his oars and plied them very carefully, but even so he could hear the lion bumping against the boat. Robert was so afraid of breaking the lion that he held his breath every time he heard a bump.

Then he heard a call from the shore. There was Aaron, standing under the horse-chestnut tree where Robert had first seen Jobi.

Robert headed for the tree, rowing slowly. When he was near enough to be heard, he called out, "Aaron! Run down to that tree trunk that's in the river. I've got something here."

Aaron ran to the fallen tree trunk and waited until Robert brought the boat close to the shore. "What have you got?" Aaron asked.

"I've got a lion," Robert answered.

"A lion!" exclaimed Aaron. "Is it drowned?"

"No," replied Robert. "It's a wooden one."

"Oh," said Aaron.

"Can you help me put it in the boat?" Robert asked.

"Sure," said Aaron. "Wait until I put my violin down."

Aaron placed his violin case on the ground, and Jobi sat down on top of it.

"You better sit on the tree trunk," said Robert, "so you won't fall in the water."

Aaron sat down and his bare feet dangled into the water. Robert pulled on the rope that was fastened around the lion's paws. "Now, if you can reach in and get hold of his head," said Robert, "I'll take hold of this piece that is on the bottom. Then we can get it into the boat." Aaron reached into the water and took hold of the lion's head, and Robert took hold of the base of the figure. "Now, heave!" Robert called out.

Aaron pulled up the lion's head, and Robert lifted the base. In a moment the lion was lying in the

bottom of the rowboat. "Come on in the boat," said Robert to Aaron.

"I have to get my fiddle," said Aaron. Aaron ran back and picked up his violin case and put Jobi on his shoulder. From the trunk of the tree he handed the violin case to Robert. Jobi needed no invitation to get into the boat. He jumped in, and Aaron followed him.

Sitting in the boat, the boys leaned over the wooden figure and looked at it carefully. "Well, what do you know," said Robert. "This is the British Lion that we've fished out of the river."

"The British Lion?" Aaron exclaimed.

"Yes," replied Robert. "You know. The lion stands for Britain, the way the eagle stands for the United States. I know that, because my grandmother is an American."

"Oh," said Aaron, as his hand reached out to touch the lion. While the boys examined it Aaron's hands played over it lovingly. Finally he said, "I never saw anything like this before. Somebody must have whittled it. My granddadda used to whittle the best clothespins any Romany ever saw, but he couldn't have whittled a British Lion."

"Let's take it to Mr. Lovell and show it to him," said Robert.

Robert rowed back to Mr. Lovell's dock and tied up the boat. The boys climbed out and they ran to the workshop. "Mr. Lovell!" said Robert. "You must come and see what we have in the rowboat!"

"It's a bit of whittling, Rai, like I've never seen before," said Aaron.

The boys led the way back to the dock. They all crouched down on the dock and looked into the boat. Mr. Lovell let out a low whistle. Then he said, "My! Oh, my! What a beautiful piece of carving! That should be worth quite a bit of money. A fine British Lion."

"I'll have to advertise and say I've found it," said Robert.

"Of course," Mr. Lovell agreed.

"You mean maybe you'll have to give it up?" said Aaron in surprise.

"Yes," said Robert.

"But you didn't steal it," said Aaron. "You found it in the water and pulled it out. Just like a fish."

"You see, Aaron," said Mr. Lovell, "this is valuable, and when you find something that is valuable, you have to try to locate the owner."

"Oh," said Aaron. "What if you can't find who it belongs to?"

"Well, then, Robert can keep it," said Mr. Lovell.

The wrinkles in Aaron's forehead cleared, and he said, "Oh, I hope he can keep it, 'cause I never saw such good whittling. I wish I could do whittling that good." Aaron reached into his pocket and, very shyly, pulled something out. "I like to whittle," he said. "I whittled this from that piece of wood you gave me the other day. I made it for you, Rai." Aaron handed Mr. Lovell a carved flower.

Mr. Lovell held it carefully and, as he looked at it, he said, "Why, Aaron. Did you make this?"

"Yes, Rai," Aaron replied. "I like to whittle."

"Why, this is beautiful, Aaron," said Mr. Lovell. He held it out for Robert to see.

"Oh, boy!" said Robert. "Wait until the twins and Daisy see this."

Now Robert was anxious to show his newfound treasure to his mother, so he said, "I guess we'll have to have our lessons tomorrow."

"Okay," Aaron replied.

Chapter Seven

LESSONS

Two rainy nights had driven Robert out of his tent and into his bed in his own room. It continued to rain for two more days, and Robert began to wonder when he would be able to go out on the river again. He could not meet Aaron in the field below Mr. Lovell's as long as it rained. On the third afternoon a watery sun broke through the clouds, but the willow trees continued to drip and the canvas covers remained on the Spencers' motorboat as well as the rowboat. A week passed before the sun had dried the countryside.

Robert's father had put an advertisement in the paper telling of the finding of the carved lion, but so far no one had telephoned. As the days passed Robert felt more and more certain that he would be able to keep the lion. He had placed it on the chest in his room and, during the rainy days, he had run into the room again and again to look at it.

Finally a warm sunny morning came, and Robert again carried a pile of books down to the dock and put them in the rowboat. It seemed a long time since he had seen Aaron.

Soon Robert was rowing downstream, keeping close to the shore. As he approached the bend in the river, he began to wonder whether Aaron would be waiting for him in the field. But the moment he rounded the bend he heard Aaron's voice calling out, "Robby! I'm here."

When Robert reached the big horse-chestnut tree he saw Aaron standing under it. He was holding the old violin case. Jobi came running down the bank when he saw Robert in the boat. "Jobi's glad to see you," Aaron called.

"I wasn't sure you would be here," Robert called back. "I'll be right there as soon as I tie up the boat at Mr. Lovell's dock. I've got the books here."

Robert turned the boat about and rowed back to the dock. He placed the oars in the bottom of the boat and made it fast. Then he put his books on the dock, climbed out, picked up the books, and carried them through the hedge that separated Mr. Lovell's garden from the big field.

"Are they the books that I'm going to learn to read?" asked Aaron, as Robert put them down under the horse-chestnut tree.

"Yes," replied Robert. "I think you will like these."

"That's an awful lot of books," said Aaron. "Where did you get so many books?"

"Oh, I have a lot more," said Robert. "You see, I like to read."

Aaron looked down at the books at his feet. After a moment he said, "But what will I do if I like to read? I don't have any books."

"I'll lend you mine, Aaron," said Robert. "You can read all of my books."

Aaron knelt down beside the books. He picked one up and held it in his hand. He looked up at Robert, and said, "But when I go away in the *vardo,* what will I do?"

"I'll give you a book to take with you," said Robert.

Aaron began turning the pages in the book he was holding. He saw some pictures in it. "Oh, pictures!" he said. "I like pictures." He looked all through the book, and when he closed it, he said, "I could never tell what all those black letters mean. Never!"

"Oh, yes!" said Robert. "You have to learn to read, Aaron. You've got to. It's easy."

"Well, I'll try," said Aaron.

Robert sat down under the tree beside Aaron. He opened the book. "Now you look at each word as I point to it," said Robert, "and I'll read."

"Uh-huh," said Aaron.

Robert began. He read slowly, " 'There was once an old witch—' "

Aaron pointed to the word. "Is that *witch?*"

"Yes, that's *witch,*" Robert replied.

"I like witches!" said Aaron.

Robert continued, " 'She lived in a little house which stood in the middle—' "

Aaron stopped Robert again and pointed to the word *which*. "You said the other was *witch,*" he said.

"Well, there are two," said Robert.

"Two witches?" said Aaron. "I thought it said, 'There was once an old witch.' Did you read it wrong? Are there two old witches?"

"No," said Robert. "There's only one old witch."

"Well, what kind of a witch is this?" Aaron asked, pointing to *which*.

"Uh, well, you see," said Robert, "this *which* is the one that stood in the middle of the forest."

"Oh," said Aaron, "then there were two witches, the witch that had the little house and the witch that stood in the middle of the forest."

"No! No, Aaron!" said Robert. "There was only one witch. You see, this *witch* is spelled w-i-t-c-h, and this *which* is spelled w-h-i-c-h."

"Oh," said Aaron. "Now show me again which is the witch that lived in the little house." Robert pointed to the word *witch*. "Now see if I can point to the one that stood in the forest," said Aaron.

"But Aaron," Robert tried to explain, "this *which* is a different kind."

"You mean one witch is a bad witch and one is a good witch?" Aaron asked.

"Aaron," said Robert, "there is just one witch.

Just one! This other *which* is telling where the house is." Robert pointed with his finger and read again, " 'She lived in a little house which stood in the middle of the forest.' "

"Oh," said Aaron. "I see, but it's hard, ain't it?"

"No. It's easy," said Robert, moving his finger to the next word, and reading, " 'Whichever—' "

He hesitated a moment, and Aaron said, *"Whichever*—is that the witch's name?"

"No!" Robert cried. "Aaron, don't interrupt or you'll never learn to read!" Robert went on reading, " 'Whichever way she looked she could see nothing but the tall trees.' " Robert stopped. "Now, Aaron. You read what I just read."

Aaron looked startled, and said, "I can't! There are too many witches in it, and I get the witches all mixed up."

"I thought you liked stories about witches," said Robert. "I picked this book out especially because it was about witches."

123

"Well, I like to hear about witches," said Aaron, "but I don't like to read about witches. They get me all mixed up. Maybe I better show you how to play the fiddle."

Robert was glad to lay the book aside. "All right," he said.

Aaron opened the violin case. He lifted the violin and the bow out of the case and handed them to Robert. Then he lifted off the handkerchief that was around his neck, and said, "You have to put this *diklo* under your chin before you put the fiddle under your chin."

"Why?" Robert asked.

"Because you might spit on the fiddle," said Aaron.

"I don't spit on things," said Robert, "and I wouldn't spit on your fiddle."

"Well, you might," said Aaron, tucking the handkerchief under Robert's chin.

"I never spit on anything in my whole life," said Robert, "and I'm not going to spit on your fiddle."

"I know you wouldn't spit on it on purpose," said Aaron.

"Course not," said Robert, placing the violin under his chin. "Now what do I do?"

"You see these strings?" said Aaron. "Well, you have to put your fingers on them near the top."

"Put all of my fingers on all of the strings?" Robert asked.

"No. One finger on one string," Aaron replied.

"What for?" said Robert.

"Because it makes the fiddle sound different," said Aaron. "Now, do it and make the bow go."

"Do what?" Robert asked.

"Push on the string with one finger," said Aaron, "and pull the bow."

Robert pressed down on one string and drew the bow across the violin. There was an ugly squeak. "What made it do that?" asked Robert.

"You didn't do it right," said Aaron.

"No wonder I didn't do it right," said Robert. "I

can't see for this handkerchief. What do you call it?"

"A *diklo*," replied Aaron. "I'll fix it for you." Aaron straightened the handkerchief.

"I could play it if I didn't have to have that thing," said Robert. "I don't know why I have to have it."

"I told you. So you don't spit on the fiddle," said Aaron.

"Are you sure that's what it's for?" Robert asked.

"My dadda told me that's what it's for," said Aaron, "and my granddadda told me that's what it's for. My granddadda said, 'Be careful of your fiddle! Don't let any old Gypsy play it without a *diklo* under his chin.' He said, 'Like as not he'll be chewing tobacco, and he'll spit on your fiddle.' "

Robert looked right into Aaron's face, and said, "But I don't chew tobacco! My father doesn't chew tobacco, and my grandfather doesn't chew tobacco. I don't know anybody who chews tobacco, and I'll never learn to play the violin with this thing under my chin!"

"All right," said Aaron, "give me the *diklo*." Aaron pulled the handkerchief out from under Robert's chin, and Robert sneezed. A little spray landed on the violin.

"See!" said Aaron, wiping it off with the handkerchief. "You spit on it."

"No, I didn't!" said Robert. "I just sneezed on it. I'm sorry. I didn't mean to do it."

Aaron took the violin from Robert and stood polishing it.

"You know what, Aaron?" said Robert. "I think it's hard to learn to play the violin."

"Oh, no. It's easy," said Aaron, "but I think it's awful hard to learn to read."

"Tell you what let's do," said Robert. "I'll read to you and you play the fiddle for me."

"Will you read about witches?" said Aaron.

"Sure," Robert replied.

Robert settled himself against the trunk of the horse-chestnut tree, and Aaron squatted on the ground beside him. Aaron held his fiddle on his knees. Jobi sat in his usual place on Aaron's shoulder. Robert picked up the book and began to read, " 'There was once an old witch. She lived in a little house which—' "

Aaron plucked softly on the strings of his fiddle.

Robert felt in his pocket and pulled out the roll of gumdrops. He held it out to Aaron. "Have a gumdrop?" he said.

"Thanks," said Aaron.

"Take one for Jobi," said Robert.

Aaron gave a gumdrop to Jobi. For the next hour Robert read to Aaron. Then Aaron played the fiddle for Robert.

When Robert heard the town clock strike twelve, he closed the book and said, "I have to go home now." As he was packing up his books, he said, "I like to hear you play your fiddle. I'd like you to play for the twins and Daisy. I want them to hear you too."

"I won't do it!" said Aaron. "I won't play for those Gaujos! I told you I don't like Gaujos."

"You like Mr. Lovell, don't you?" said Robert.

"He's different," said Aaron.

"I think if you knew the twins you would like them," said Robert. "And I think you would like Daisy. We have a lot of fun in the pool and in the tree house. And do you know what?"

"What?" said Aaron.

"I'm not going to sleep in my tent anymore. I've decided that I'm going to sleep in the motorboat. If you would like to come some night, there's room in the motorboat for you, too. How about it?"

"Maybe," said Aaron. As he walked away, he turned and said, "Thanks, Robby."

Chapter Eight

A NIGHT IN THE MOTORBOAT

LATE one afternoon Robert's father discovered that there was something the matter with the motor on the motorboat. Robert sat on the dock watching his father tinker with the motor. At last his father said, "I can't fix it. I'll have to take it off and have Mr. Lovell fix it. He knows all about motors."

Mr. Spencer brought his tools from the boathouse and unfastened the motor. Robert helped him lift it onto the dock. "I'll put it in the boathouse," said his father. "Tomorrow I'll take it over to Mr. Lovell."

That evening at dinner Robert's father said to him, "It should be a fine night tonight, Robert. The moon will be full. Are you planning to sleep in the boat?"

"Oh, yes," replied Robert.

"Robert will be sound asleep," said his mother, "long before the moon comes up."

"Maybe I'll wake up and see it," said Robert.

It was still daylight when Robert was ready for bed. He came out to the garden, where his father and mother were sitting, dressed in his striped pajamas. His arms were filled with a large quilt. "You'll come down to see me, won't you?" he said.

"When you're settled we'll come," said his father.

"I'll say good night now," said Robert. "I might just be asleep when you come." Robert kissed his father good night, and then he kissed his mother.

"Be sure of your mooring," his father called after him, as Robert ran down to the dock. "Be sure your ropes are well fastened."

"Oh, sure," Robert called back.

When he reached the dock he threw the quilt into the boat. Then he jumped in. His sleeping bag was there, covered with a sheet of plastic to keep it dry. Robert removed the sheet of plastic and poked it under the back seat of the boat. Then he spread the quilt over his sleeping bag, in case it turned cold during the night.

Robert stepped into his sleeping bag and poked his feet down into the cozy lining. Then he pulled up the zipper. He punched his pillow and settled his head. He yawned and closed his eyes. This moment was one that Robert loved. Half-asleep, he could feel the gentle rocking of the boat and hear the quiet lap of the water. Voices carried from an occasional boat as it passed by. A sea gull screeched.

Soon Robert's father came. He stooped down on the dock and looked into the boat. "All tucked in, Robert?" he said.

"Hm-m-m," Robert replied.

"Good night, Son," said his father.

"Night, Daddy," Robert murmured.

Robert knew that his mother would come soon. He would try to stay awake. He could hear someone strumming a guitar in a passing boat. It was a tune Robert knew. He began to hum to keep himself awake until his mother came. Through his drowsiness he half remembered that he had not tested the ropes that moored the boat, but he was too cozy to get out now. After all, they were always all right.

A few minutes later, when his mother came and looked into the boat, Robert was sound asleep. "Good night, Robert," she said. "Good night, dear." There was no reply. The clock on the town hall struck nine.

No sound from the river disturbed Robert's sleep. Robert's father and mother sat in the garden while the long twilight faded. They watched the full moon rise and grow brighter as darkness came. It made a path of brilliant gold across the river and bathed the garden with a blue-white light. The white flowers seemed brighter by moonlight than they did when the sun shone upon them. At last, Robert's father and mother went into the house. His father locked the doors. Before very long the house was dark.

The boat, moored to the dock, shone like a silver shell on the water, and the willow tree was a shimmering curtain when Aaron walked up the garden path to Robert's house. He had walked in the moonlight from his father's wagon to Robert's gate. He had had no trouble in finding it, for it was as light as day. Jobi was on Aaron's shoulder.

Aaron was surprised to find the house unlighted. He had left his mother baking a cake in the campfire. Romany friends had arrived. The night had just begun for the Romanies. His father had taken up his

fiddle, and while the cake baked there would be sing-
ing and, perhaps, dancing until daybreak. Aaron
knew that he would not be missed. It was a good
night to go and sleep in the boat with Robert.

Aaron moved cautiously when he reached the
dock. He stooped down and looked into the motorboat. There was Robert, sound asleep. One hand was
under his cheek. The other rested outside of his sleeping bag. Aaron watched his quiet breathing. The
moonlight lay full upon Robert's face. Aaron could
even see his long pale eyelashes turned to silver in the
light. He looked down at Robert for a long time. He
had never seen a child asleep before, for he had no
brothers or sisters. The sight of Robert so still, the
gentle rocking of the boat, and the flicker of the
moonlight on the water filled Aaron with peace.
He longed to get into the boat and lie down beside
Robert, but he could not bear to wake him.

Meanwhile, Jobi was running hither and thither
on the dock. He climbed down and jumped around

on the old automobile tires that were fastened to the dock to keep the boats from scraping against the rough wooden boards. Then he swung back and forth on one of the ropes that moored the motor-boat to the dock. Robert slept on, undisturbed. In a few minutes the monkey dropped from the rope and ran along the edge of the boat to the stern. There was another rope that fastened the boat to the ring on the dock. But Jobi could not swing on this rope, because part of it dipped below the surface of the water.

At last Aaron took his eyes from Robert and looked around for Jobi. The monkey was sitting hunched over, stiff and still, as far out on the stern of the boat as he could get. He was sitting right where the motor had been, looking down into the water. Aaron heard Jobi make a sound, low in his throat. Then he uttered a faint cry. "Shush!" Aaron whispered.

Still looking into the water, Jobi chattered.

"Shush!" said Aaron again. "Come!" he whispered. Jobi didn't move. Aaron knelt down on the dock and reached out for Jobi. "Come here!" he whispered.

The monkey chattered and scratched at the rope. Something in the water was exciting Jobi, but Aaron did not look down into the water. He just reached out and caught hold of Jobi. "Do you think I'm going to wait all night while you look at the fish?" he whispered, as he carried the monkey to a spot under the big willow tree.

Aaron was used to sleeping on the ground, so he lay down on the bank under the willow tree. He had worn an old coat, and with it he covered himself. Jobi lay down beside him and soon they were both asleep.

Only an occasional boat passed on the river now. The police patrol launch went by as the town clock struck one.

As three o'clock chimed, Jobi woke up. He lay for a while playing with his hands and his feet. Then he got up and walked around Aaron several times, but Aaron was sound asleep. Jobi wandered out to the dock, where he walked up and down. Then he jumped and grabbed hold of the rope that held the prow of the motorboat fast. The boat rocked a bit, but Robert did not stir. Jobi was wide-awake and the moonlight made him feel frisky. He ran along the edge of the boat back to the stern and looked down into the water. A water rat lifted its head and looked into the monkey's beady eyes. Then it scuttled away.

Jobi grabbed the rope that hung over the side of the boat and gave it a hard pull. It came up out of the water. It was a short piece of rope, and the end was frayed. This rope, which had held the stern of the boat, was no longer fastened to the ring in the dock. The water rat had gnawed through the rope and cut it in two. The piece that was tied to the dock now hung straight down into the water.

The monkey soon tired of playing with the short piece of rope. He dropped it and ran back to the prow, where he could swing on the other rope. He hung by his thin hairy arms and swung his legs back and forth. Suddenly he fell on the deck of the boat, and the rope fell with him.

Jobi picked himself up and pulled on the rope he was holding. It was no longer tight. He ran out to the edge of the prow to see if he could find the rope on which he had been swinging. He looked all around, but he could not find it. He did not know that the limp rope in his hand was the rope that he had been swinging on.

The town clock struck four and a faint light was showing in the east when the police patrol launch passed again on its way down the river. The wake from the police boat rocked Robert's bed, but he was in a deep morning sleep. Shortly afterward Robert's boat began to move. Very slowly it moved away from the dock. Soon it was caught up in the current of the river and was floating downstream. It passed Mr. Lovell's place and the field where Robert had first seen Aaron and Jobi. The current carried the boat farther and farther, past the quiet houses on the banks of the river.

Daylight came. A loud alarm clock rang out from a house close to the shore. It made Jobi jump, but it did not waken Robert. Soon there were signs of life around the houses. Doors banged and radios could be heard announcing the morning news. Robert stirred. He rubbed his eyes and turned over for another snooze, but something did not seem quite right to him. He was used to the boat rocking, but it wasn't rocking now. Suddenly Robert was aware that the boat was moving. He sat up. The first thing he saw was a monkey sitting on the prow of the boat. Robert rubbed his eyes. He wondered why he was always seeing monkeys. Then he looked around. He saw a house on the bank of the river, but it was not his house. He looked at the opposite bank. There were houses there, but none that Robert had ever seen from his own dock.

Robert crawled out of his sleeping bag. He climbed

up on the back seat of the boat. The monkey turned and looked at Robert, and Robert decided that it must be Jobi. But if Jobi was here Aaron should be here, too. Where was he? Had he fallen into the river? Robert looked around. What were they doing out here in the river? He looked at the monkey, and said, "What happened?" But Jobi could not tell him, and he did not seem to care. The monkey seemed to be enjoying his boat ride.

Robert wondered how he could get back to the dock. He had never run the motorboat, but with no one here to run it for him, he would have to try to do it himself. He had often started the motor for his mother, so that was the first thing to do. Robert looked at the stern of the boat—and then he remembered that his father had taken the motor off to have it repaired. Now he knew that he was really adrift. He had no motor and not even an oar.

The motorboat continued to drift downstream in wide circles. Robert saw one side of the river, then the other side of the river. Now he was looking up-stream, and now downstream. Wherever the current took the boat, Robert and Jobi traveled.

Robert looked at the boats tied up along both sides of the river, but there was no one in any of them. Where is everybody? Robert wondered. The river had always seemed so full of boats, going up or down. Now it seemed as if every boat on the river had been laid up for repairs. Even though it was early in the morning, there should have been a few boats out.

Then a sailboat appeared, tacking upriver. Robert's heart rose. Maybe the people on it will help me! he thought.

As the sailboat came nearer Robert saw that there were two big boys in it. "Hey, booby!" one of the boys shouted. "What do you think you're doing?"

"Get off the river before somebody runs you down," the other boy called out.

"I can't!" Robert called back. "I'm adrift!" But at that moment the wind changed and the sailboat almost turned over. The boys were too busy handling it to pay any attention to Robert.

Robert caught a glimpse of the stern of the sailboat. It was named *Our Own*. Robert thought the name was very strange, and he noticed it had been painted by someone who made bad letters.

The boat drifted on, and before long Robert could see the lock ahead. This sight comforted him a little. If the boat is carried to the lock, the lockkeeper will see me, thought Robert. Then the lockkeeper will send someone to give me a tow. But his thoughts grew dark again, for he thought of the dam. If the boat was carried to the left he would reach the safety of the lock, but if it drifted to the right he would go to the dam. Robert knew that there was a barrier to keep boats from going over the dam. But because all river traffic went through the lock, he realized that he might rest by the barrier a long time before anyone discovered him.

Robert watched carefully as the boat drifted. If

only the current would carry him to the lock. It was too soon to tell. He tried to push the boat to the left, but before very long his hope faded, for he saw that he was drifting toward the dam.

Robert began to wonder how long it would be before his father and mother would know that he was adrift. He wondered again where Aaron was. He was worried about him. How could Jobi look so contented? Didn't he miss Aaron? Didn't he care anything about Aaron? Maybe he had seen Aaron fall off the boat and drown, and still he sat there on the stern of the boat as contented as a sea captain. A dog would worry and whine for his master, but Robert thought that this old monkey must have a marble for a heart.

The sun was up now, and Robert could see an occasional boat heading for the lock, but either the people in the boats were just looking toward the lock or they were too far away to see that Robert's boat was adrift.

Robert watched the boats as they lined up to enter the lock. He stood up and waved his arms, but no one seemed to pay any attention to him. When he saw the boats begin to move he knew that the lock was open. One by one the boats disappeared. When the last one had gone, Robert watched anxiously to see if any would come upstream through the lock. If one came, it might sight him over by the dam. Looking through the barrier he could see the water going over the dam.

Suddenly what should he see but the police patrol launch coming out of the lock! Robert stood up and waved both of his arms. He called out as loudly as he could, although he knew that they were too far away to hear him.

No sooner had the police boat appeared than Robert saw it turn and come toward him. Now he was so excited he waved harder. It was all he could do to keep from jumping up and down. "I'm adrift!" he called. "I'm adrift!"

As the boat drew nearer, Robert knew that the

police had seen him. He heard them throttle down the motor. Then one of the policemen called out, "We've come to give you a tow. Can you catch the rope when I throw it?"

"Oh, sure!" Robert replied.

The policeman threw the rope, and Robert fastened it to the boat. "Thanks," he said.

"Your father called us," said the officer. "He caught us at the lock."

"I guess you were surprised when you woke up out in the river," said the other patrolman.

"I sure was!" replied Robert. "This boat doesn't even have a motor."

"I guess you'll get quite a welcome when you get home," said the policeman.

The police launch towed the motorboat up the river, and before long Robert saw his own dock. He could see his father and mother in their bathrobes, and Aaron was there, too. Robert was glad to see Aaron. They were all waving their hands.

When the police launch maneuvered Robert's boat up to the dock, one of the officers said to Robert's father, "Well, sir, here's your sailor!" Looking at Robert's pajamas, he added, "We don't often find them in striped uniforms."

Everyone laughed as Robert's father tied up the boat.

Jobi was the first to hop out of the motorboat. "There goes the admiral," said the other policeman. "He was on watch out there on the stern." Aaron picked Jobi up and patted him.

When Robert stepped out of the boat he ran to his mother, while his father tested the mooring lines. "How did you know I was adrift?" he asked his mother.

"Aaron was sleeping in the garden. He woke up and saw that the boat was gone," she said. "He came pounding on the front door and wakened us."

Just as the police launch was about to leave, one of the officers said to Mr. Spencer, "By the way, I think

I should tell you that there are some Gypsies in the neighborhood. Better keep your boats well moored. They disappear on this river every once in a while. We're looking for a sailboat now. All very mysterious, you know." The men waved and the police launch was off.

Robert ran to find Aaron, but Aaron and Jobi had disappeared.

Chapter Nine

MORE ABOUT JOBI

THERE was a stiff breeze on the river one morning when Robert rowed across to pick up Daisy and the twins. He had not seen them for over a week. They were all waiting for him when he pulled up at the dock. Daisy had a bag of currant buns to eat in the tree house.

"Hello, Robby," Timothy called out.

"Where have you been so long?" Jeffrey cried.

"We've missed you," said Daisy, handing the bag of buns to Robert before she stepped into the boat. "Have you found any treasures?" As she sat down, she said, "How is your friend Aaron?"

"He's fine," replied Robert.

"Does he still have the monkey?" asked Jeffrey, settling himself.

"Of course," replied Robert, as he picked up the oars.

"Have you ever seen his wagon?" Timothy asked.

"Of course," said Robert.

"Did you see the inside?" Daisy asked, with a little shudder.

"Sure, I did," replied Robert, pulling away from the dock.

"Ooo! I'd be afraid," said Daisy.

"What is there to be afraid of?" asked Robert.

"Oh, I don't know," said Daisy, "just Gypsies and the monkey and everything. It would make me come all over queer."

"Come all over queer!" Timothy repeated. "What kind of English is that? You're talking like a Gypsy yourself."

"Well, you know what I mean," said Daisy. "Feel funny, that's what I mean."

"What was it like, Robby?" Timothy asked. "What's a Gypsy wagon like inside?"

"It's like a playhouse," Robert replied, "a wonderful playhouse. If I could just have a Gypsy wagon, I would think it was the best thing in the world."

"Well, if you had one," said Jeffrey, "where would you keep it?"

"Oh, I know where I would keep it," said Robert. "I'd keep it out by the garage."

"And you'd let us come and play in it, wouldn't you, Robby?" said Daisy.

"I thought you didn't like Gypsy wagons," said Timothy.

"I'd like it if there weren't any Gypsies in it," said Daisy.

When Robert reached the other side of the river, he said, "Do you want to go downriver a bit?"

"Oh, yes," said Jeffrey. "Maybe we'll see the monkey."

Robert rowed past his own dock and past the houses that lay between his dock and Mr. Lovell's. As he passed Mr. Lovell's dock, Timothy said, "We heard about Mr. Lovell's sailboat being stolen. Do you know anything about it, Robby?"

"No," replied Robert. "It's a mystery."

As Robert neared the bend in the river, he heard, very faintly, the music of Aaron's violin. Daisy sat up straight and looked around. "I hear music!" she said.

"I do too," said Timothy. "Somebody's playing a violin."

"It's pretty," said Daisy.

Robert lifted his oars and the rowboat floated idly.

"Aren't you going around the bend, Robby?" Daisy asked.

"Let's wait a minute," said Robert.

"Who do you suppose is making that music?" said Timothy.

Robert looked at his three friends, and said, "I know who it is. It's Aaron."

"Aaron!" Daisy cried. "Can Aaron play the violin?"

"He sure can," Robert replied.

While the children listened, Robert's eye was caught by a sailboat out in the middle of the river. It was manned by two big boys. They looked familiar to Robert. As he watched them, the wind changed suddenly and the boat dipped far, far over. Suddenly Robert cried out, "Look!"

The children turned and looked where Robert was pointing. They heard the boys shouting. Then they saw the two boys go over the side of the boat. The next moment the sails touched the water and the bottom of the boat appeared. For a few seconds the boys couldn't be seen, but then Timothy cried out,

"There they are! They're swimming toward the opposite shore."

"Yes!" Jeffrey cried. "They're leaving the boat!"

The children in the rowboat watched the boys reach the shore and clamber out of the water. Then they saw them run as fast as their legs could go along the towpath.

A passing motorboat had gone over to the capsized sailboat, but the people in the motorboat didn't seem able to do much about it.

Suddenly Robert shouted, "Here come the river police!" He took up his oars, and as fast as he could he rowed to Mr. Lovell's dock. When he reached the dock, Mr. Lovell was standing there, watching the police. They now had the sailboat upright.

"Mr. Lovell!" Robert called out. "Mr. Lovell! Did you see what happened?"

"I did," replied Mr. Lovell. "I've been watching those boys with that boat through my binoculars for some time."

"Do you think it's your boat that was stolen, Mr. Lovell?" Timothy called out.

"I don't know," Mr. Lovell replied. "The police will probably bring it over here."

"Can I tie up, Mr. Lovell?" Robert asked.

"Yes, of course," said Mr. Lovell, taking his glasses down. "I'll tie you up."

In a few moments the four children were on the dock, waiting for the police to tow the sailboat over to Mr. Lovell. They were so busy watching the police launch that no one saw Aaron standing back by the hedge with his fiddle under his arm and Jobi on his shoulder. Jobi's arms were around Aaron's neck.

A moment later Daisy turned, and when she saw Aaron she gave a little start. She stared at Aaron and the monkey. Then she tucked her hand into Mr. Lovell's and took a tight hold. She looked up at him, and said, "There's the Gypsy."

Mr. Lovell turned, too, and when he saw Aaron he called out, "Hello, Aaron! Come on over."

As Aaron came near, Daisy's grip tightened on Mr. Lovell's hand. He leaned down, and said to her, "The monkey won't hurt you, Daisy. He's a tame little fellow."

"Hi, Aaron!" Robert called out. "These are my friends. That's Daisy and this is Jeffrey. He likes monkeys. And this is Timothy. Did you see what happened to that sailboat out there?"

Aaron said a quiet "Hi" to Robert's friends. Then he said, "I saw."

Soon the police launch was towing the sailboat toward Mr. Lovell's dock. They towed it very slowly, because it was full of water. As they came near, one officer called up to Mr. Lovell, "Do you think this could be your sailboat?"

"Could be," replied Mr. Lovell. "I'd have to look it over to be sure. If you can inch her up, I'll tie her."

"We'll pump the water out of the boat," said one of the officers. "We have a pump."

Robert, Jeffrey, and Timothy all tried to help Mr.

Lovell, and they all got in Mr. Lovell's way, but he managed to tie up the boat without anyone falling off the dock. Only Aaron and Daisy were quiet. They stood still. Daisy looked at Aaron out of the corner of her eye, but she didn't go near him.

As soon as the sailboat was fast the police began to pump the water out of it. When they had finished, Mr. Lovell jumped down into the boat. He looked it all over. Finally he said, "It certainly looks like my boat. This badly painted name on the stern looks as though it might have been painted by a young boy."

"*Our Own* is a strange name for a sailboat," said one of the officers.

"Sounds as if they were trying to prove to everyone on the river that they owned it," said the other officer.

Mr. Lovell continued to examine the boat. At last one of the policemen said, "What do you think, Mr. Lovell?"

"I'm pretty certain this is my boat," he replied.

"Unless you can find something about it that makes you absolutely sure that it's yours, we'll have to take it up to headquarters," said the policeman.

Mr. Lovell looked up at Aaron and laughed. "Aaron," he said, "I shouldn't have removed all of those blue paint marks." Mr. Lovell had no sooner finished speaking than Jobi jumped from Aaron's shoulder. As quick as a flash Aaron handed his violin and bow to Daisy and ran after Jobi.

Jobi liked to be chased, and he was in the mood for a chase. He ran up and down the dock. "Come here!" Aaron cried, but Jobi paid no attention. He jumped up and down and squealed with delight.

"He's showing off," said Robert.

Just as Aaron was about to catch Jobi, the monkey jumped into the bottom of the sailboat. "Oh, there goes the admiral again," one of the officers on the police launch called out. In a flash the monkey had disappeared under the deck of the sailboat.

"Well, what about this boat, Mr. Lovell?" asked

the officer. "Do we tow it into headquarters? Of course, the boat could belong to those boys. They may have been too frightened to stay with it. If they come up to headquarters and can show evidence that it's theirs, we'll have to hand it over to them. Isn't there some definite proof that this boat is yours?"

Aaron was down in the sailboat now, looking under the deck where Jobi was hiding. Suddenly he cried out, "Rai! It's your boat! Some of that blue paint from Jobi's feet is still here!" Aaron was now holding Jobi in his arms.

Mr. Lovell knelt down and looked under the deck, and there he saw the smudge of blue paint. "This is it, officer!" Mr. Lovell called up to the men on the police patrol boat. "This is my boat. I can tell, thanks to this monkey." Then Mr. Lovell told the officers how Jobi had run all over the boat and left footprints that had to be removed with turpentine.

The policemen laughed and started their motor. "Well, that's one mystery solved," an officer said.

"The next thing is to track down those boys who stole it." Then the police launch moved away from the dock.

"I'm greatly obliged to you," Mr. Lovell called to them.

Mr. Lovell helped Aaron and Jobi out of the sailboat, and the other boys gathered around Aaron and his monkey.

"Now the monkey is sort of a hero, isn't he, Mr. Lovell?" said Jeffrey.

"I guess it was a good thing Jobi got the blue paint on the boat after all," said Robert.

"I'm going to telephone to London and tell the man who bought the boat that it's been found," said Mr. Lovell.

Daisy, with Aaron's violin and bow still in her hands, came nearer. Suddenly she surprised Robert by saying, "Aaron, we heard your music. I think it's wonderful! Will you play some more for me?"

Aaron put Jobi down and took his violin and bow

from Daisy. He placed the violin under his chin and began to play. One by one the children sat down on the dock. They listened quietly to Aaron's playing.

Mr. Lovell had gone back to his house, but as Aaron played the last note, he returned. "I have just telephoned to London," he said, "and I told the owner the whole story about his boat and about Jobi." Mr. Lovell turned to Aaron. "What do you think the man said?"

"What?" shouted the children in a chorus.

"He said, 'Now I know what I shall name the sailboat! I'll name it *Jobi*.'"

The children laughed, and Robert cried, "That's wonderful."

Aaron looked pleased and Daisy clapped her hands. "I told you he was a hero!" said Jeffrey.

"It's an honor to have a sailboat named for you," said Timothy. "It's too bad Jobi can't read and see his name on the sailboat."

Robert quickly changed the subject from reading,

167

and said, "I guess we better be going. Aaron, you come with us."

Aaron hesitated. "Come on, Aaron," said Jeffrey.

"Yes, come on," Timothy added.

"We're having currant buns in the tree house," said Daisy. "I brought some extra ones this morning."

Aaron looked at Daisy, and he saw that she was trying hard not to be afraid of Jobi. "I'll come," he said, "but not in the boat. I'll walk by the road."

"Okay," said Robert, "see you later."

The four children got into the boat, and Mr. Lovell untied it. They rowed off while Mr. Lovell walked to the gate with Aaron. As they were walking through the garden, Mr. Lovell said, "How did you get along with your reading lesson, Aaron?"

"Aw," said Aaron, "I'll never learn to read. Never."

"Would you like to learn?" Mr. Lovell asked.

"Sure," said Aaron, "like Robert. He reads so good. All those stories!"

"Would you like to go to school?" Mr. Lovell asked.

"Oh, school ain't for Romanies," said Aaron. "We'll be leaving soon now. The picking's almost over."

The two reached the gate. Mr. Lovell opened it, and said, "You'll come see me again before you go?"

"Oh, sure, Rai," said Aaron. "I'll come back. Will I see Jobi's name on the boat when I come back?"

"I'm going to paint it on as soon as I scrape the other name off," replied Mr. Lovell.

A wide smile spread across Aaron's face and his white teeth flashed. "I'll like seeing that, Rai!" he said.

When Aaron reached Robert's willow tree that held the tree house, Robert called out, "We're up here, Aaron. Come on up!"

Aaron looked at the ladder that he would have to climb, and he said, "I'll leave my fiddle down here." Aaron ran to the porch and placed his violin and bow on the porch table. Then he went back to the tree.

"Are you going to leave your monkey down there, too?" Daisy called.

"Oh, no!" Jeffrey cried. "Bring the monkey up."

"Maybe the monkey would like to sit in the tree basket," said Daisy.

Robert leaned over and called down, "Put Jobi in the basket, Aaron, and I'll pull him up."

Aaron placed the monkey in the basket, and Daisy said, "Maybe Jobi would like to swing in the basket. It would make a nice swing for him."

"Pull him up!" cried Jeffrey. "Pull him up, Robby."

"I think Jobi would like to swing," Aaron called.

"You mean you want me to pull him about half-way up?" Robert asked.

"Yes," said Aaron. "About halfway up."

Robert pulled on the rope, and, when the basket was halfway up, he tied the rope to a branch of the tree. Aaron climbed the ladder and looked down at the monkey. Jobi was swinging back and forth, enjoying the new game.

Every once in a while, Daisy looked down at Jobi. Once she dropped a piece of her currant bun, and it fell right into the basket. She watched the monkey as he ate it, and said, "He's cute, Aaron. I never had any monkey friends, but I think I could be friends with this monkey."

Aaron untied the rope from the tree. He pulled the basket up, but Jobi screamed when Aaron tried to lift him out of the basket, so there was nothing to do but let the basket down again. Jobi continued to swing back and forth until it was time for the children to go home.

Aaron waved to Daisy and the twins as Robert set off with them in the rowboat. The children waved back. As Aaron picked up his fiddle and bow, he said to Jobi, "Gaujos ain't so bad, Jobi."

Chapter Ten

BACK TO SCHOOL

O<small>NE</small> afternoon Robert rode off on his bicycle to visit Aaron, for he had seen nothing of Aaron for over a week. As he approached the woods where he had found the Gypsy *vardo,* he watched for the first glimpse of the blue wagon. In a moment he was surprised to see something red gleaming through the trees. Robert rode faster until he reached the woods.

He got off his bicycle and stood still. He did not have to go farther to see that an old black car and a red trailer were standing under the trees. There was no sign of the blue Gypsy wagon.

Robert leaned his bicycle against a tree, and began to shout, "Aaron! Aaron!"

The door of the trailer opened and Aaron came out. "Hi, Robby," he called, as he came toward Robert.

"Aaron!" Robert cried, running to meet him. "Where's the wagon? Where's the wagon?"

"It's still here," said Aaron. "It's around on the other side of the trailer. You can't see it because the trailer hides it. My dadda's going to sell it. He sold the horse last night."

"I want to see the wagon," said Robert. "I want to see it."

"Don't you want to see the trailer?" said Aaron.

"No. I want to see the wagon," Robert replied.

Aaron led Robert around to the other side of the

trailer. There was the wagon, looking small beside the trailer. "It's empty," said Aaron. "Everything's in the trailer now. The poor *vardo!* I was going to whittle flowers and stick them all over it. I can't whittle flowers and stick them on the trailer."

"Oh, Aaron!" Robert exclaimed. "I want this wagon! I want it!"

"What for?" asked Aaron, looking surprised.

"I want it for a playhouse," Robert replied.

"A playhouse!" said Aaron. "You've got a play-house up in the tree."

"But this would be different," said Robert. "I could sleep in it, and when you come back next summer you could sleep in it, too. Just think, Aaron! You'd be coming back to sleep in your old *vardo!* And you could make your flowers and stick them all over the wagon, and it would get more and more trimmings."

Aaron's eyes seemed to grow bigger and bigger as Robert talked. "But you'd have to buy the *vardo,*" said Aaron. "How are you going to buy it?"

"I'll ask my father to buy it," said Robert.

"Do you think he will?" Aaron asked.

"I don't know, but I'm going to ask him," Robert replied.

Then Aaron took Robert into the trailer and pointed to an empty shelf. "That's where I aim to keep my books."

"Oh, Aaron," said Robert. "You're going away before I've taught you to read, but I'll give you one of my books to put on your bookshelf."

"Thanks, Robby," said Aaron. "I hope it has pictures."

"I'll give you one with pictures," said Robert.

"You know something?" said Aaron. "Mr. Lovell was here last night. He came to see my dadda about something."

"Oh! You don't think Mr. Lovell is going to buy the wagon, do you?" said Robert.

"I don't think so," Aaron replied. "I heard him say something about my learning to read. I heard my dadda make a big row at first, but the Rai just went on talking quietly. When the Rai went away, I looked out the window and I saw them shake hands. I don't know what they were talking about, but I think it was about me."

Robert didn't stay very long, for he was anxious to get back home. When he told his mother about the wagon, she said, "We shall have to see what Daddy thinks about it."

"You do think it would be nice to have a Gypsy wagon, don't you, Mummy?" Robert asked.

"I think it would be very nice," his mother replied, "but Daddy will have to decide."

"Mr. Lovell was up to see Aaron's father last night," said Robert. "You don't think he is thinking of buying the wagon, do you?"

"I don't know what Mr. Lovell would want with a Gypsy wagon," his mother replied.

"You never can tell about Mr. Lovell," said Robert. "Maybe he wants to buy a horse and go

Gypsying. There's *something* he's thinking about, or he wouldn't have gone to see Aaron's father."

When Robert's father came home that evening, Robert sat on the arm of his chair and told him about the Gypsy wagon. His father listened to everything Robert said about the wagon, then he said to him, "You do seem to pick up the most unusual 'all sorts.' Other boys bring home shells or collect stamps, but you find wagon wheels and monkeys and lions, and now you want to bring home a Gypsy wagon. It's all very peculiar, Robert."

"But you do think it is nice peculiar, don't you, Daddy?" Robert asked.

"I'm not so sure," his father replied. "The Gypsy wagon will probably cost a lot of money."

"But it's the only 'all sort' that has cost anything, Daddy," said Robert. "You know, the wheels I found helped to build my wagon Kronk. And after all, the lion must be very valuable, and no one has claimed it."

"Very well," said his father, "we can sell the lion and buy the wagon."

"Oh, but Daddy!" said Robert. "I have plans for the lion. I thought I would fasten the lion over the door of the wagon."

"Really, Robert! You can think of the most unusual uses for things," said his father.

"Well, Daddy, what do you think?" said Robert. "Shall we get the wagon?"

"We'll take a look at it this evening," his father replied.

"Jolly good!" said Robert.

Early in the evening Robert and his father and mother set off in the car to look at the Gypsy wagon. Robert showed them the way, and soon the car turned into the woods. "I never would have believed that I'd ever buy a Gypsy wagon," said Mr. Spencer, as he stopped the car.

Aaron had heard the car, and he came running to meet them. He led them to the trailer where his father and mother greeted them. Then they all walked around the trailer to look at the wagon.

At first Aaron's father made believe he didn't want to sell it, and Robert's father made believe he didn't want to buy it, but both fathers knew Gypsy business. For fifteen minutes the price of the wagon went up and the price came down. Then it went up a little bit and then it came down a little bit. Finally the two men agreed upon a price. Aaron's father clapped his hand against Mr. Spencer's hand, and the wagon was sold.

Everyone went into the trailer, and while Robert's father paid for the wagon Aaron's mother brought out little cakes and tea.

When Robert and his father and mother said good-bye, Mr. Spencer said, "I'll see about picking up the wagon. I'll probably come for it tomorrow evening." The three Gypsies flashed wide smiles and everyone shook hands.

Not long after the Spencers had left, Aaron's

father said, "Come, Aaron. We'll take the wagon to your nice friends."

"Oh, yes, Dadda," said Aaron.

Soon the Gypsy wagon was rolling along the main road. Aaron's father pulled one of the shafts and his mother pulled the other. Aaron pushed from behind. When they passed Mr. Grimes's store, Mr. Grimes said to Mrs. Grimes, "There go those Gypsies. Wouldn't you think they would get themselves a horse?"

"Funny people, Gypsies, I always say," said Mrs. Grimes. "Do you suppose they're going to pull that wagon all over England?"

"Couldn't say," said Mr. Grimes. "The Spencer boy was in one day. Said he'd like to have one of those Gypsy wagons. Can you imagine that?"

"Funny boy, that Robert," said Mrs. Grimes. "Notiony."

Robert and his parents were in the garden when there was a knock on the front gate. Robert ran to open it, and, to his great surprise, there were the Gypsies with the wagon. "Mummy! Daddy!" he cried. "They're here with the wagon!"

Robert's parents hurried to the gate. When Mrs. Spencer saw Aaron's father and mother pulling the wagon, she said, "Oh, you shouldn't have done this! You must be worn out, pulling that heavy wagon."

The Gypsies laughed. "It's nothing," said Aaron's father. "We're strong people."

Robert opened the gate wide. Then the Gypsies

pulled the wagon through the gate and placed it behind the garden wall.

"Do come into the house," said Robert's mother, "and let me give you a cold drink. You must be very warm." But the Gypsies refused.

Robert couldn't wait to climb into the wagon. He looked down from the door, and said to Aaron, "Now when you come back next summer, you'll come back to your own *vardo.*"

Aaron looked at his father, and they looked as though they shared a secret. "Shall I tell Robby, Dadda?" Aaron asked.

His father nodded.

"I'm not going away," said Aaron. "My folks are going without me. Mr. Lovell's asked my dadda to let me stay with him so I can go to school."

"Oh, Aaron!" Robert cried, jumping down from the door of the wagon. "Aaron! That's super! You'll learn to read!"

After the Gypsies had departed, Robert ran to the

motorboat where his sleeping bag was. He took it out of the boat and carried it across the garden. He dragged it up the steps and into the wagon. His father and mother watched him, and his father said, "I never knew anyone who made his bed in so many different places. In the tent he's an American Indian, in the motorboat he's a sea captain, and in the wagon I suppose he's a Gypsy."

"He hasn't slept in the tree house yet," said his mother.

"He will," said his father, "he just hasn't thought of it. When he does he'll probably take a flashlight along and be a lighthouse keeper."

The following week Aaron's father and mother set off on their travels. They were very proud of their car and trailer, but they no longer looked like Gypsies.

Aaron and Jobi had already moved into Mr. Lovell's house, where Aaron had a little bedroom like Robert's. His father and mother stopped to say good-bye to Aaron and Mr. Lovell. Then they all stopped at Robert's house and said good-bye to Robert and his mother. They were sorry Robert's father was away at work.

Aaron's father started the car, and Aaron and Mr. Lovell and Robert and his mother began to wave good-bye. They waved their hands until the trailer disappeared around a bend in the road.

When Robert's holidays were over and the day arrived for him to return to school, he ran ahead of his mother toward the dock. He was looking forward to taking Aaron with him to school. When he saw Aaron waiting on the dock he was surprised, for Aaron was no longer wearing his bright shirt and his green trousers. He was wearing flannel shorts, with carefully pressed creases, and a jacket. His mop of black curly hair was covered with a small blue cap just like Robert's. Although Robert had known that Aaron would wear the school uniform, he was not prepared for the big change in Aaron's appearance. For a moment Robert felt that he was meeting a new boy, but when he heard Aaron's voice call out, "Hi, Robby! Jobi cried when I left him," Robert felt that this new Aaron was still his old friend.

"Oh, he'll be all right," said Robert, as he untied the boat.

"I hope so," said Aaron. "I don't want him to give the Rai any trouble."

When Robert's mother reached the dock, she said, "Good morning, Aaron."

Aaron had noticed that in Robert's world everyone said "Good morning" to everyone else instead of nodding their head, so Aaron said, "Good morning."

Robert held the boat while his mother and Aaron got in. Then Robert jumped in after them. When the boys were settled in the boat, Mrs. Spencer picked up the oars. "I suppose Mrs. Wiggins will be waiting for us," Robert remarked.

"I'm certain she will be," his mother replied.

As the rowboat moved from the dock, they passed close enough to the great willow tree for Robert to reach out and pull a leaf from the branch that skimmed the water. A little yellow color was now showing where before the leaves had been dark green.

As they rowed across the river, they passed a large group of swans. Aaron said, "Are those the Queen's swans?"

"Probably some of them are," replied Robert's mother, "but many are not. Swans are swans, you know."

"Yes," said Robert, "the Queen's swans and the other swans all get along together. The swans don't know who they belong to, do they, Mummy? They just belong to the River Thames."

"That's right," said his mother.

"Just like us, Aaron," said Robert. "You and I. We both belong to the river now."

CAROLYN HAYWOOD is distinguished both as author and illustrator of children's books. Her first book was published in 1939. Since then she has had twenty-five other books published and has become one of the most widely read American writers for younger children.

Carolyn Haywood was born in Philadelphia and still lives in that city. She is a graduate of the Philadelphia Normal School and studied at the Pennsylvania Academy of Fine Arts, where she won the Cresson European Scholarship for distinguished work. Miss Haywood calls herself a "grand-pupil" of the great American illustrator, Howard Pyle, having studied with three of his distinguished pupils, Elizabeth Shippen Elliott, Violet Oakley, and Jessie Willcox Smith. She is also a portrait painter and has specialized in portraits of children. Her experience in this field has given her a sympathetic understanding of children and their interests, which has made her peculiarly well fitted to write and illustrate for them. She is continuing her portrait work with commissions in New York, Philadelphia, and other eastern cities.